What was it about Ryan that dug so deep under Kellie's skin?

As they drove in silence, Kellie studied him. Ryan Marsh had a classic hero complex. No wonder he took his fiancée's accident so hard. A guy like him would torture himself over not preventing it from happening.

Overprotective? You better believe it.

Overbearing? Yes, ma'am.

And way too easy to look at.

"You can let me out here," she said as he turned down her drive.

He kept going.

"Did you hear me?" she asked.

"Yeah, but I'd just as soon see you get in the door safe and sound."

Yep, ridiculously overprotective.

Again, the image of him as a gallant knight ready to slay a lurking dragon flitted through her mind. Ryan reminded her of what she'd always dreamed of—a prince who'd rescue her from the darkness. She quickly shook away those girlish thoughts. She'd learned that fairy tales didn't come true and had the scars to remind her of that.

Books by Jenna Mindel

Love Inspired

Mending Fences
Season of Dreams
Courting Hope
Season of Redemption

JENNA MINDEL

lives in northwest Michigan with her husband and their two dogs. She enjoys a career in banking that has spanned twenty-five years and several positions, but writing is her passion. A 2006 Romance Writers of America RITA® Award finalist, Jenna has answered her heart's call to write inspirational romances set near the Great Lakes.

Season of Redemption
Jenna Mindel

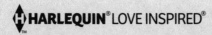

Recycling programs
for this product may
not exist in your area.

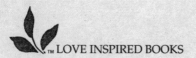 ™ LOVE INSPIRED BOOKS

ISBN-13: 978-0-373-87864-2

SEASON OF REDEMPTION

Copyright © 2014 by Jenna Mindel

www.Harlequin.com

Printed in U.S.A.

To all who mourn in Israel, He will give: beauty for ashes; joy instead of mourning; praise instead of heaviness. For God has planted them like strong and graceful oaks for His own glory.

—*Isaiah* 61:3

I'd like to thank everyone who gave me such rich insight into the world of counseling, social work and substance abuse treatment. To Kelly Kippe, Becky Ledingham, Jeffrey Seltzer, Megan Grodesky and Steve Mindel—thank you for your time and generous wisdom. To Officer Jason Traeger, thank you for answering my many questions about possible arrest situations without thinking I'm a kook!

I really appreciate the great resources you guys have been for me. I hope this story rings true, and if it doesn't, I take full responsibility.

To my critique partners, Kathleen Irene Paterka and Christine Johnson, thank you for keeping my characters honest. You helped bring more depth to them and for that I'm so grateful.

To my new editor, Shana Smith, who is a delight, we're going to make a great team!

Chapter One

Kellie Cavanaugh rushed into the office bringing with her a blast of chilly autumn air and a few colored leaves that had blown against the door. She was late. Not a good thing considering she interned for LightHouse Center, a substance abuse outpatient office in LeNaro, Michigan. She wanted a good report despite her tardiness.

Grabbing a quick cup of coffee, she took a sip and coughed. "Ugh, who made this?"

Marci, the receptionist, laughed. "John."

"What's wrong with my coffee?" Her boss, John Thompson, stood with hands on his hips.

Kellie made a face. "It's like tar."

"Get here on time and you can make the coffee." His voice sounded stern, but Kellie knew better. John was all bark.

Still, she managed a sheepish smile. "Sorry I'm late. I overslept."

John nodded. "How'd your interview go yesterday?"

Kellie had left early to interview with the large school district in Traverse City. One of their school counselors had tendered her two weeks' and needed to be replaced. The school was currently interviewing. John knew the school's superintendent and had pushed to get her in the door. She owed him big-time.

"Promising. Very promising." Kellie added more cream and sugar to the super strong coffee.

Again, John nodded. "Ginny's not here today, so I'd like you to take this morning's assessment. It's a court order and the guy's waiting in the lobby."

Kellie peeked at the tall, dark and handsome man pacing the tiles. "You want me to take *him?*"

"Yes, I do. We're all part of a team. When one of us is missing, others fill in. Besides, you've done well with our teens. I think you're ready."

She was ready. With only a month left of her internship, Kellie had been doing teen assessments on her own. She'd even facilitated the teen group sessions for the last few weeks. Kellie had shadowed her mentor, Ginny, for months. She knew how to conduct an adult assessment. She'd seen it done by the best.

Still, Kellie didn't appreciate the way her heart pounded. Was it normal nerves or something else? She peeked again at the guy in the lobby and a flutter of attraction rippled through her.

Nope, not going there.

The guy moved with impatient grace, like some fairy-tale prince who'd lost his way to the castle, but he was no storybook hero charging in to give Kellie a happily-ever-after. Kellie didn't believe in fairy tales anymore. She believed in hard work and faith in God to get a person where they wanted to go.

"Here's the alcohol screening questionnaire he completed. Looks pretty clean." John handed her Prince Impatient's paperwork. "It's his first offense."

"You mean the first time he's been caught." Kellie scanned the documents for his name. *Ryan Marsh.*

John gave her a tsk-tsk of warning. "Careful, Kellie, you haven't been here long enough to be that cynical."

Kellie shrugged. Her cynicism had been cultivated long ago. She flipped through Ryan's papers. He'd been court-ordered for a substance abuse assessment as part of his conditional sentence for Operating While Visibly Impaired. A misdemeanor. It didn't matter that he'd been hit with the lowest charge; the guy had been arrested for an alcohol-related crime. In her book, that made him a modern-day leper—treat with compassion but do not touch.

"Okay." The lobby seemed to shrink before her eyes. She could do this. She knew how to control her reactions and her feelings. She'd done it for years.

Kellie glanced at Marci, sitting primly behind a sliding glass window that gave her an eyeful of Prince Impatient's delectable pacing. "Give me a minute and then send him back."

"Sure thing, Kellie." Marci snapped her gum and gave her a wink.

Kellie took a steadying breath, picked up her doctored coffee and headed for her office. It was one thing meeting with kids, quite another to assess someone so handsome it hurt to look at him.

After five minutes of mental prep, she looked up to see her Prince Impatient literally darken her doorstep. If a person could look like a thundercloud personified, it was definitely Ryan Marsh.

"Come in, Ryan, please. I'm Kellie Cavanaugh, an intern here." She extended her hand hoping he didn't notice the way her voice had cracked.

He briefly returned her handshake.

Kellie didn't cower at his strength or the fact that he towered over her. "Have a seat."

He sat down, his knees brushing the front of her desk.

So far, he hadn't said a word, but she could feel his frustration and something darker emanating from him like a low growl. Shame? This bear of a man had been caught in his own snare.

"So, tell me why you're here."

His eyes widened slightly, and he wiped his palms against long, jean-clad thighs as if it took considerable effort to remain seated. His impatience hadn't cooled as he gestured toward the paperwork on her desk. "You've got the court order."

"Yes, I do. But I'd like to hear your story."

"It's so stupid." His deep voice sounded remorseful rather than defensive.

Most stories she'd heard here were, but Kellie didn't say that. She nodded for him to continue.

"How long will this take? I've got to get to work."

Ryan had a job that he was worried about keeping. Definitely a good sign. Same with his questionnaire. He'd given a lot of right answers, but that didn't mean they were true.

"About an hour or so. I have a series of questions to ask, so you might as well get comfortable."

He nodded but didn't relax.

"You were about to tell me what happened," Kellie coaxed.

"I was at a party and had a few beers too many—" His gaze pierced her. "Something I don't usually do. Anyway, a friend agreed to drive me home. While I was waiting for him in my truck, I must have dozed off. The police were called because of the noise, and the next thing I knew I was arrested."

Kellie studied him. Hard. Something didn't add up. He didn't usually have a few too many beers? *Right.* A person didn't get arrested without cause. "What happened to your friend?"

"He bailed on me."

Classic.

She sat back. "Do you hang out with this friend a lot?"

Ryan shook his head. "No. We went to high school to-gether. I ran into him at a football game, and he invited me to the party and I went. He hadn't been drinking and agreed to drive me home."

"In your truck?" Kellie had heard all kinds of lame excuses sitting in on assessments. This one was right up there.

He ran his hand through thick dark hair that had a nice wave to it. "Yeah. I know. Stupid."

"So the police arrested you because…?" She wanted his perspective on why he'd gotten into trouble.

"It was cold that night, so I started the truck to turn on the heat. I was sitting in the passenger seat, but it didn't matter. The cops said I had control of the vehicle with the intent to drive."

"And did they talk to your friend?"

"No. They couldn't find him. He left with someone else and that's all it took to make me out as a liar."

Was he? A twisting worm of doubt in her gut said he wasn't. Maybe he'd been at the wrong place at the wrong time under the wrong circumstances. "This is how you remember it happening?"

He looked her straight in the eye. "That's how it hap-pened. I had no intention of driving. I don't drink and drive."

Kellie shifted under that direct gaze, but she didn't look away. His eyes were dark brown and hard like bitter choco-late. That worm of doubt turned again. Liars weren't usu-ally so forthright.

She cocked her head. "Okay, tell me about yourself. Who are you, Ryan?"

The corner of his eye twitched. "What do you want to know?"

He did things the hard way. Okay, fine. "I have an entire sheet of questions here, which we'll take in order. The more open you are, the easier this will be."

"I don't have a drinking problem," he said.

He wouldn't be here if there wasn't something amiss in his life. "A problem is a broken shoelace, something you fix and it goes away. We treat the disease of alcoholism and addiction. That requires management skills."

This time he shifted in his seat, looking wary. Nervous even. "Okay, what's your first question?"

"Your general health appears good. Are you currently taking any prescription meds?"

"No."

"Have you ever been prescribed medications for pain?"

"Yes."

Kellie narrowed her gaze. "When and what were they?"

"I had my wisdom teeth pulled a month ago—they were impacted pretty bad. I still have the bottle of Percocet."

"Did you take them?"

"I took one."

"Why only one?"

Ryan shrugged. "I didn't like how it made me feel."

"And how did it make you feel?"

"Sort of loopy." He sat forward with an annoyed look on his face and his dark brows furrowed. The thundercloud was back. "Look, Ms. Cavanaugh. I don't do drugs. I never have. And I don't normally drink much."

How many times had she heard her brother deny his addiction? How many times had her parents believed him? They refused to see what his substance abuse did to their family.

What it did to her.

She cleared the painful memories inching into her brain. Ryan Marsh was convincing. He believed he was okay, and part of her wanted to believe that, too. He wasn't like her brother. For one thing, Ryan looked a person in the eye.

"Except for that party?"

He sat back and blew out his breath in frustration. "Yeah, except for that party."

She'd hit a nerve but had to dig deeper. "Why?"

Now he looked angry. "What do you mean, *why?*"

"Why did you have a few beers too many?"

He looked away then and shrugged. Now he *was* lying. By refusing to admit his reason, he wasn't being true to himself or to her. Ryan Marsh had a definite purpose in drinking that night, she was certain. He didn't strike her as the kind of guy to do anything by accident.

She waited, feeling the struggle going on inside him. "Ryan?"

He looked up.

In his eyes she read stark pain so acute, her heart flinched. It felt like she'd run into a jagged piece of glass that cut quick and deep. "Alcohol won't make it go away."

"It did for a while."

Her stomach tipped over and fell, feeling like it had dropped to the soles of her feet. Ryan Marsh hurt, and he hurt badly. People hurting that bad often tried to medicate their sorrow to make it go away instead of dealing with it. Is that what he was doing? Was this the first stepping stone to a bigger issue?

Please, God, no...

The prayer whispered from her soul. She often prayed for clients, especially the teens in her group. She cared, but this was different. This bordered on something else. A connection between them where she felt his pain and wanted to take it away. But she couldn't do that. Things didn't work that way.

Straightening her paperwork, Kellie regrouped. This man wasn't her client nor would he be. She was only filling in for Ginny. Ryan Marsh would become an agency client if recommended for counseling. She needed to remain impartial, objective and, above all else, emotionally removed.

But those eyes of his were killers, sucking her into a vortex of feelings she shouldn't have. Settling the list of standard questions on the desk in front of her like a shield, she continued her line of questioning and note-taking.

His employment, his education, his family life—everything checked out. He was a regular guy with a normal life. From what he'd told her, a very stable life. Ryan was the middle child of three. He grew up on his family-owned cherry orchard, but he worked as a farm manager for a nearby horticultural research station. He'd worked there since graduating from college five years ago. The guy had no prior arrests, not even one speeding ticket according to the court records.

Yet, he was here.

She looked at him. "So, you've never been in trouble with the police before."

He fidgeted in the chair and his boot hit the front of her desk when he tried to cross his legs. "Sorry."

Again she'd hit a nerve. Had he been in trouble before? She smiled and waited for him to answer.

"I'm sorry, what was the question?"

She rephrased. "Have you ever been in trouble with the police before? Maybe not arrested, but warned? Or questioned?

The color drained from his face. "Questioned."

"Why?" She held her breath.

"My fiancée was killed in a tractor rollover. My brother

and I were there when it happened." A brief glimpse of that tragedy shone from his eyes, but then he shuttered it off as easily as she might pull the shades on a window.

"When was this?"

"A little over three years ago." He looked down at his feet. With his elbows balanced on his knees, Ryan clasped his hands so tight his knuckles had turned white.

She watched him closely. It was eating him up inside. Was he an alcoholic without knowing it or headed there because of his grief? It wasn't uncommon for someone who'd never showed signs of substance abuse to slide down that slippery slope as a way to cope.

"I'm sorry for your loss."

"Yeah, me, too." He struggled for control.

Part of her wanted to dig deeper, get him to talk about what had happened that day, but she stopped herself from asking the question poised on her lips. She wasn't his counselor.

Kellie quickly gathered her papers and stood. "I think I have everything I need for now. You signed a permission waiver for us to check with your family, so I'll complete those interviews later today."

He stood as well. "Why do you have to talk to them? I told you everything you asked."

Kellie wouldn't sugarcoat the reason. "We need to establish your credibility."

He jammed his hands in his pockets. "Okay, fine. Then what?"

"Then I'll review what we discussed along with the questionnaire you completed and make my recommendation to my boss and mentor counselor. Once they've reviewed the paperwork, we'll forward their findings to the court. You'll get copies of everything."

Ryan looked worried. "When will I hear something?"

"By the end of the week." She extended her hand. "I know this isn't easy on you, but we're on the same team."

Ryan took it and squeezed.

For a moment, Kellie didn't think he'd let go. His touch wasn't threatening at all. In fact, all the bluster had gone out of him and he hung on like she was a rescue ring tossed in rough waters.

When he finally did let go of her hand, Kellie was tempted to reach for him again. And that was plain old crazy thinking. And dangerous.

He headed for the door and then stopped, turned around and gave her a hint of a smile. "Thanks."

"You're welcome." Kellie's heart pounded all over again.

Ryan stepped out of the treatment center into cold October sunshine peeking out from behind dark gray clouds. He felt a lot like the dried-up leaves getting swirled into a circle in the parking lot. His whole life had been stirred into a mess of decayed matter.

What had he gotten himself into? One stupid decision had cost him way more than the money spent on court fees, increased insurance and an invasive assessment. Despite the promise of dropped charges once he satisfied the conditions of his sentence, namely an evaluation and possible treatment, this thing had the power to impact the rest of his life.

Clicking the unlock button on his keys, Ryan climbed in his truck, but he didn't start the engine right away. He stared at the trees on the surrounding hills that blazed in bright hues of orange and red. He'd made two stupid decisions. The first had been letting Sara try that asinine stunt with the tractor.

If only he'd told her no…

He leaned his head back and sighed. "I am such an idiot."

The night of the party would have been their third wedding anniversary had Sara lived. They would have been married three years, maybe with a baby on the way. Ryan briefly closed his eyes. The pain hadn't gone away. The hollow feeling he carried around had grown like a cancerous tumor.

He'd tried to recover through church, then isolation, and then that night, he'd tried something else. The party had given him an excuse to go further than a few beers to relax. He'd effectively blurred his memories until he couldn't recall them anymore. He'd drunk enough to blot out that look on Sara's face when she lay in his arms, dying.

It had been a real treat for his family to find out he'd been arrested. His one call had been to his future brother-in-law instead of his parents. Adam had picked him up from jail without lecture, but it was still a humbling experience he'd never want to repeat. Not something he'd wanted to place on his parents, either. Knowing his mom, she might have left him in jail overnight to think about what he'd done to get there.

That pretty intern reminded him a little of his mom. Kellie Cavanaugh wasn't exactly short, maybe more average in height, but she looked small and delicate despite her powerhouse of a handshake. With light freckles all over her face and eyes that couldn't decide whether to be blue or green, she'd nailed him with a direct gaze that saw far more than he'd wanted her to see. A good talent when it came to counseling, but potentially bad news for him.

He wasn't a drunk. But would Kellie Cavanaugh see that? He wanted this whole thing done and over with, but his future lay in her hands. He started his truck and slammed it into Reverse.

By the time he got to work, Ryan was glad his duties today included fall cleanup in the cherry fields. Throwing stuff around sounded good right about now.

"How'd it go?" His boss, Liz, stood in the doorway of his small office.

"I don't know. I'll find out if I have to go to 'treatment'—" Ryan made quotation marks with his fingers "—by the end of the week."

Liz gave him a smile. Only a few years older than his twenty-seven years, Liz was hired in as the new director of the research center six months ago when she moved back to the area with her husband.

She'd been great through this whole thing, promising to go to bat for him if record of his arrest printed in their local newspaper was ever questioned by the board of directors.

"Have you thought maybe this is what you need?"

"I don't abuse any substance—" He cut himself short. Was that true anymore?

Liz held up her hand. "You're the most dependable, hardworking guy on staff, but there's this sadness in you…. I know it's about your fiancée, but maybe this is all for some big cosmic reason."

Ryan snorted. "You sound like my brother."

"Well, maybe we have a point."

"Yeah, well. I've got stuff to do. Thanks, Liz." Ryan wasn't interested in a theological debate. If he heard one more time from well-meaning folks how *all things work together for good to those who love God*, he'd tear his hair out.

How could God use *this* one? Ryan had blocked out God for a while now. Maybe He'd finally received the message and had given Ryan a hands-off. And look where he'd landed.

* * *

Two days later while waiting for her evening teen group session, Kellie sat at her desk with her office phone cradled against her shoulder. "Mrs. Marsh? Hello, this is Kellie Cavanaugh from the LightHouse Center in LeNaro. Do you have a few moments?"

She heard a sigh at the other end.

"Yes, I do. Ryan told me you might be calling." Ryan's mother had a pleasant-sounding voice.

Expecting the call was another good sign. Ryan Marsh demonstrated responsibility by giving his family members a heads-up. Or he could have prepped them on what to say. Either way, Kellie would find out.

She'd hit a wall with his evaluation. She believed what Ryan had told her even though her boss thought his answers were too perfect to be true.

Was Ryan headed for trouble? If he remained on this course, most likely he would be. She'd spoken to Ryan's brother, a minister, who had shed a lot of light on the accident that had killed Ryan's fiancée. Her name was Sara, and she'd died in Ryan's arms. Kellie nearly cried after she'd hung up.

"Mrs. Marsh, I was wondering if I might ask you a few questions about your son."

The chuckle on the other end of the phone surprised her. "Mrs. Marsh?"

"Oh, please call me Rose. And sorry, but this is just so unusual."

Kellie tipped her head. "How so?"

"It's not like Ryan to do anything wrong. When the boys were younger, I used to get all kinds of calls about my oldest son, Sinclair. But he's settled down and recently married. Ryan was always the responsible one."

Rose Marsh sounded vibrant and proud of both her sons.

There wasn't that weary tone in her voice, like she'd been through the wringer over and over again. Interesting.

"Does Ryan have a history of abusing alcohol?"

"No, not really. In fact, Ryan was the type of kid who'd call me fifteen minutes before his curfew with the reason why he might be late. I never worried about Ryan in that respect."

"Rose, if I may ask, is there anything that worries you now?"

"His grief." Another sigh. "He's not moving on, and it's been three years."

"Yes, he told me about that. I'm very sorry for your loss."

"Thank you, Miss Cavanaugh."

"Kellie."

"Can you help him, Kellie?"

She felt her back stiffen. "I'm not his counselor. I'm helping with the evaluation."

"He'd have a fit if he knew I'd said this, but I want him to go through some sort of counseling. Ryan's too deep a thinker. He keeps his feelings locked up inside and wouldn't dream of seeking help on his own. And he needs help."

Still waters run deep with dangerous currents and undertows.

"Kellie?"

"Yes, ma'am?

"Do you believe in God?"

A personal question for sure, but Kellie wasn't surprised or offended. Ryan's brother was a pastor, and he'd told her that they'd been raised in a Christian home. The Marsh family had been more than simply Sunday morning churchgoers. They tried their best to live their faith. Like her.

Kellie cleared her throat. This call was taking an unexpected turn. "Yes, ma'am, I do."

"There's an old poem that refers to God as the Hound of Heaven. Well, I think God's tracking down my son to bring him back. Please recommend Ryan to go through counseling. He can't carry his burden of grief anymore. He needs to finally give it over to the Lord, before he lets it destroy him. Do you know what I mean?"

"I do, Mrs. Marsh." A little too well, in fact. Some things were hard to let go of.

After a few more questions, Kellie hung up the phone. God worked in mysterious ways, but this one really confused her. Was she supposed to be God's instrument in this man's life? That was a big responsibility. One she didn't take lightly. A knock on the door to her tiny office interrupted her thoughts, so she hit the save button on her computer.

Ginny stuck her head around the door. "Do you have that Marsh evaluation done yet? John's asking for it. He's got a relatively new group starting up and can take on another client."

"It's right here." Kellie hit the print button and then pointed at the shelf. "Or rather, there."

"Great. Let's review it before our teen group session, okay?" Ginny gathered up the pages and scanned them quickly. "Heard anything from the school yet?"

"Not yet. I don't expect to for a while." Kellie sat on her hands to keep them still while Ginny settled into a chair. She gave her time to read the report thoroughly.

"So, you believe this guy's telling the truth?" Ginny's gaze narrowed.

"I do."

Ginny smiled. "You're so young."

Kellie knew that was her mentor's way of saying naïve.

One of the things Kellie had learned interning here was that the counselors were pretty skeptical. They had to be.

"And yet you're recommending a minimum amount of counseling. Why?"

Kellie wouldn't admit that Ryan's mother had asked her to, or that she'd confirmed Kellie's thought process. "I think he might be headed for real trouble if he doesn't deal with his emotional pain."

Ginny rolled her pen between her fingers. "*Might* being the operative word here. Do you think he's an alcoholic?"

"Most of the signs point to no." But Kellie had her doubts.

The way he'd admitted to a reprieve that night at the party, the night he'd been arrested, raised a red flag. Ryan Marsh had found a destructive way to cope.

Kellie knew all about that.

Ginny gave her a hard stare of consideration. "Okay. I'm approving it. John will be happy for a solid self-pay, and maybe we can prevent this guy from going down the wrong road."

"Exactly." Kellie nodded, but she felt like she'd betrayed Ryan.

A guy like him wasn't going to be happy with the news. Nope. Not one bit.

Chapter Two

How'd he get here? Really, how had this happened? Ryan took a seat in one chair of many that made a circle. The group session room at LightHouse Center looked sterile and cold despite the inspirational posters on the walls and potted plants on the windowsills.

Some of his fellow group members were a little rough around the edges. The young woman to his left might as well be a walking billboard for the tattoo shop in town. Another guy had a beard that shouted Willie Nelson impersonator. Seriously, they looked like they belonged here. He didn't. And he had weeks of this to look forward to?

Clenching his jaw, Ryan glanced around. Where was that pretty intern? He wanted to tell her she'd made a big mistake. He'd read that report, and yeah, there was some scary truth to what she'd written, but that didn't mean he needed this. He definitely didn't want it..

He watched more people roll in and take their seats. Normal-looking people, professionals even. So far, thankfully no one he knew.

"I think we should get started." John Thompson, the guy he'd met with briefly after hearing the verdict of his assessment, also sat down in the circle.

"We've got several new people," John announced. "I'd like to go around the room and have everyone introduce themselves and state why you're here. First names only. Everything said here stays here. Confidentiality and anonymity are crucial to the safety of the herd."

Ryan would give anything to wring that intern's neck. What color would her eyes turn then? The thought made him smile. And then he heard the silence and realized the group was waiting for him.

He slid back in his chair and wiped his hands on his jeans. "I'm Ryan and I don't get why I'm here."

The woman with the tattoos gave him a sarcastic once-over, like *he* was the loser. A couple of folks snickered.

"Okay, Ryan. Eventually, you will." John didn't like his answer. No surprise there.

John hadn't liked any of his answers when they'd met to map out his master treatment plan. Ryan's goal was getting this over with as soon as possible and meeting the condition of his sentence so the charges would be dropped. Period. He didn't have a problem. Not a drinking problem anyway.

Then the guy slouching next to him answered, "Yeah. My name's Pete, and what he said is good enough for me, too."

"Honesty, folks." John peered over his glasses at them before giving Ryan a pointed look. He had a short stack of papers attached to a clipboard, resting on his knee. "We'll get nowhere fast with minimized answers."

And so it went. Ryan steeled himself for the psychobabble that promised to fill his next hour and a half. By the time the group session was over, Ryan didn't linger. He didn't want to meet anyone. He didn't want to chat over coffee. He wanted out of there.

Climbing into his truck, he started the engine and pulled

out. He cringed at the squealing sound from his tires but kept driving—too fast. He had to get far away from all that. As far as he could go.

Okay, slow down and breathe. Just breathe.

A couple of miles out of town, he finally relaxed. He'd survived his first session. He could do this. He clicked the power button of the radio and fiddled with his preset tabs until he found a country station. The current song's poor-me wails had him changing the channel to a contemporary Christian station. He tapped his fingers on the wheel as he listened to the soothing sounds of a rock-styled worship song.

How many times had he sung this song in church without a thought to the words? He felt a tugging at his heart but clicked off the radio.

Why, Lord? Why is this happening?

Ryan didn't expect an answer. He didn't get one either. He wasn't exactly on solid speaking terms with the Almighty. Sure, sometimes Ryan talked—ranted usually—but rarely did he hear.

Maybe he didn't listen hard enough, but empty silence had a way of shutting down a person's prayers. Pain that wouldn't go away did that, too. Yeah, his prayers had definitely dwindled in the last couple of years.

With a sigh, he kept driving until he spotted a small car with its hazard lights flashing. A woman sat on the hood with what looked like a cell phone in her hand.

"Stupid," he muttered.

Why would a woman sit outside her vehicle on a lonely stretch of road when it was starting to get dark? All right, dusk hadn't settled yet, but it was a dark and gloomy day. He couldn't leave her all alone, so he slowed down and pulled over.

He got out of his truck and walked toward her with his

hands open in an easy manner he hoped sent the message that he was okay. He was safe. "You need help?"

"Nope. I'm good. A tow truck is on its way."

He recognized that husky, straightforward voice and stepped closer to the twenty-year-old Toyota Corolla that had a dent over the passenger side front tire. "Ms. Cavanaugh, you really shouldn't sit out here like this. Anyone could come along."

She looked up then and her eyes widened. Green. They looked green in the glow cast by his headlights. Her eyes darted nervously, too. "Ryan."

"What happened?"

She slid off the hood and stood ramrod straight. "It sputtered and died. Look, you don't have to worry. I called a tow truck."

"When?"

"Just now."

"I can't leave you out here by yourself."

"Sure you can. I'm fine." Her shoulders straightened, but she didn't look as confident as her tone sounded.

"I'll wait with you till they come. In the meantime, why don't you pop the hood and I'll take a look."

"Do you know anything about cars?" She reached inside the opened driver's side window and did what he'd asked.

"I know engines. Do you happen to have a flashlight?"

"Umm, no. Just this one on my key ring." She held up a little LED light.

"That'll have to do." He leaned over the car's engine and looked around. "Point it this way."

She did. And that brought her closer to where he stood. She smelled like fresh air and cinnamon gum.

"Does it turn over?"

"Does what turn over?" She looked confused.

Young and pretty, Kellie Cavanaugh perfectly fit the

bill for a wild Irish rose complete with sharp little thorns that cut quick. Her reddish-brown hair was pulled back in a fat braid like the day he'd met with her. The wispy spirals around her face hinted at curls. What would all that hair look like loose?

Ryan refocused his thoughts. "The car. Why don't you try and start it. Let me hear how it sounds."

She climbed in behind the wheel and turned the key. The car ignited but wouldn't start.

"That's fine." He held up his hand and then closed the hood.

She popped out of the car quick as a rabbit. "Do you know what it is?"

"Sounds like maybe your fuel pump. That's my guess."

She wrinkled her freckled nose. Definitely pretty. "Is that expensive to fix?"

He wiped his hands on his jeans. "Depends on what you consider expensive."

She briefly closed her eyes. "Let's just say the tow truck is expensive enough in my checkbook."

He watched her closely. Her clothes were basic jeans and a sweater topped with a colorful scarf wound around her neck and a flannel-lined denim jacket that looked like it had seen better days. She'd dressed similarly at Light-House Center.

He couldn't stop the offer from coming out of his mouth. "I could take a look at it for you. Might be able to save you the cost of labor, at least."

Her eyes shone with alarm and then she held up her hand. "No. Definitely not."

He cocked his head. "Why not?"

"You're a client of the agency where I intern."

"So?"

"So it wouldn't be right to take advantage of you to save a few bucks."

He laughed out loud. "Take advantage? I offered. And I don't know why considering you're the one who put me there in the first place. Why'd you do that, Ms. Cavanaugh?"

She looked down at her booted feet. "My name's Kellie."

"Kellie, then." He liked the sound of her name. Pert and to the point, it suited her.

Her movements were quick and jerky. Even standing still, she twisted the ends of that scarf with her fingers. Nervous energy or did he make her uncomfortable?

He tried again. "Why'd you recommend me for treatment?"

"This conversation is completely inappropriate."

He laughed at that, but the sound came out harsh and bitter. "Why? It's about me. I read your evaluation. You think I'm headed for, let's see, how did you phrase it? *Alcohol dependence due to a traumatic event in my recent history.*"

Her eyes flashed with defensive annoyance. "I think you need help."

He spotted the revolving red lights of the tow truck way down the road. "Yeah, well, so do you. How do you plan to get home once your car's towed to the garage?"

"I'll call…" She glanced at her watch, and her brow furrowed. "Maybe a cab."

He shook his head. No way was he letting her travel miles back to town with a greasy tow guy alone, only to sit and wait outside the closed-for-the-day mechanic's shop in town. Alone. "I live out this way. I'll give you a lift."

"No."

"Don't give me any guff about conflict of interest.

You're pinched for cash and I'm not about to let you go off by yourself. If something happened to you, I'd—" He broke off.

Her eyes challenged him. "Never forgive yourself?"

It would have stung less had she slapped him. Hard. "Yeah, that's right. Do you want to be responsible for advancing my decline?"

"Nothing will happen." But then her gaze wavered as she watched the big tow truck inch closer.

"You never know." He crossed his arms and watched her. She deserved a little fear after what she'd put him through.

Her eyes widened and a chill seemed to shake her. Cold, or maybe she'd considered the possibilities and didn't like the conclusions.

Upsetting her hadn't given him the satisfaction he'd sought. Instead, he felt the urge to wrap his arms around her, pull her close and soothe her worries. Ryan had a feeling Kellie Cavanaugh carried around too many worries.

"If anyone finds out about this, I could get in big trouble."

"What are you talking about?"

"You're a client, and I'm an intern. I shouldn't have any personal contact with you outside of a professional or community setting."

He gave her an odd look. "I'm only giving you a ride home. It's a neighborly thing to do in this community."

"It looks bad."

Ryan scanned the heavy woods on one side of the road and open fields of bare cherry trees on the other. "No one's around to see and I won't say a word, okay?"

She rolled her eyes. "Okay, fine. Give me ride."

He'd called her bluff. And he'd made her mad to boot.

The tow truck slowed to a stop with a whoosh of air and

the rattling idle of a diesel engine. If she worried about being seen with him, she might as well stay out of sight. "You're cold. Why don't you sit in my vehicle while I help this guy load up your car."

She didn't argue, even though she looked like she wanted to. Instead, she turned on worn-out work boots and headed for his truck.

He watched her. Whisper-thin, she held her chin high as she pulled open the door harder than needed and nearly knocked herself over in the process. Pert didn't begin to describe Kellie Cavanaugh, and that made him smile.

Kellie fumed while she waited. She'd been totally un-professional baiting Ryan that way. And riding home with him bordered on unethical. What was wrong with her?

She was tired. Tired from studying and even more tired of living on a shoestring budget. She glanced in the side mirror. Ryan walked toward her and the tow truck backed up. All done? That was fast.

She slipped out of the truck clutching her purse. "Wait, I need to pay the tow guy."

Ryan waved her back. "Don't worry about it. It's all set."

"What do you mean, *it's all set?*"

"I know him."

"What's that mean?" She didn't move.

Ryan gave her a harassed look. "It means what it means. Get in the truck."

"Did you pay him? Tell me how much and I'll pay you back." Cash would be better, but she didn't have anything more than a five in her wallet. She really shouldn't write a check to a client.

Ryan stood in front of her, hands on his hips. "Will you just get in the truck?"

Kellie looked up at him. There was well over six feet of

handsome man in front her and her heart took a tumble. She was supposed to be safer with him? Ha! She should have taken her chances with the tow guy.

She glanced down the road. Too late. Her car was already on its way to the only mechanic in LeNaro.

Ryan opened the passenger side door for her, and his expression softened. "Really, it's okay."

"No, it's not." She narrowed her eyes.

"Sure it is. I won't tell a soul." Ryan leaned against the door dressed in jeans and a flannel shirt over a T-shirt with the sleeves rolled up on strong forearms.

She stared at those defined muscles for a second too long before looking back into his face. He was built solid as a brick wall but she felt safe. Protected.

Weird.

The breeze rustled the fallen leaves giving the growing darkness of dusk a spooky feel. She wouldn't like walking on a night like this, that's for sure. She finally nodded and climbed back in. "Okay."

"Watch your feet," he said before shutting the door.

She fumbled with her seat belt while he slipped in behind the wheel.

"So, where do you live?"

"A few miles down this road. 3312 Lakeshore."

His eyebrows rose at the address and his expression soured.

She knew what he was thinking. Poor little rich girl living on the lake but can't afford a tow truck? Well, she didn't ask for his help and he could choke on paying her way.

Again, she gave herself a mental shake. What was it about him that dug so deep under her skin?

As they drove in silence, Kellie studied him. Ryan Marsh had a classic hero complex. No wonder he took his fiancée's accident so hard. A guy like him would torture himself over not preventing it from happening.

Overprotective? You better believe it.

Overbearing? Yes, ma'am.

And way too easy to look at.

"What?" Ryan caught her staring.

"You can turn left after the next mailbox." She pointed beyond the road, hoping to distract him from that quizzical look he gave her. Her cheeks felt way too warm.

He slowed down and then pulled into the long drive.

"You can let me out here."

He kept going.

"Did you hear me? This is good."

"Yeah, but I'd just as soon see you get in the door safe and sound."

Yep, ridiculously overprotective.

Again, the image of him as a gallant knight ready to slay a lurking dragon flitted through her mind. It was a refreshing change from what she'd been used to—guys who didn't even bother to open doors. Ryan reminded her of what she'd always dreamed of—a prince who'd rescue her from the darkness. She quickly shook away those girlish thoughts. She'd learned that fairy tales didn't come true and had the scars to remind her of that.

He slowed to a stop, but the rumbling sound of his huge truck would no doubt alert her landlady to their presence.

"Great. Now I'll have some explaining to do to Mrs. Wheeler."

"Who's she?"

Kellie savored the moment to rub his nose in her situation and wipe away his poor-little-rich-girl impression. "She's the elderly lady I live with. Rent a room from actually."

Ryan gave her a swift look of surprise. She'd scored a hit. "How are you getting to work tomorrow?"

None of your business. But Kellie smiled sweetly instead. "I have a bike."

Again, another look of surprise. "A motorcycle?"

"No. A bicycle."

He frowned.

"It's not too far to bike to town. I've done it before." Several times in fact, to save on gas money. She slipped out of the truck before he could respond. Before he could recommend a different solution. "Thanks for the ride."

Running up the walkway to the porch, Kellie turned and waved. True to his word, Ryan remained parked in Mrs. Wheeler's driveway until she slipped into the house.

"Mrs. Wheeler? I'm home." Home—yeah right.

It had been years since Kellie knew what a real home felt like. When she and her brother were little, there'd been happy times in their Grand Rapids area home. Especially at Christmas, her favorite holiday. They'd pile into the car and drive north of the city to hike into the woods and chop down a tree. Kellie and her mom took hours to decorate it. And she'd drink and eat her fill of hot chocolate and Christmas cookies.

A slender, white-haired woman peeked around the corner. "Oh. Kellie. I'm glad you made it. I started to worry."

That was nice of her, but Kellie knew better. Mrs. Wheeler was more concerned about having her home after dark so she wouldn't be all alone in her big house.

"My car broke down, so I got a ride."

"From who?" The elderly woman looked horrified.

"Someone from work." That's all her landlady needed to know.

"Good. A young girl like you can't be too careful, you know."

"True. And I am careful. Well, good night." Kellie turned to go to her rented room but hesitated when it looked like her landlady wanted to say more.

"All right then. I'm headed for bed and the TV. I'm glad you're home." Mrs. Wheeler usually made her way upstairs at nine-thirty on the dot. Every night. Tonight, she was early. Surely, the woman hadn't worried herself sick. Kellie wasn't used to anyone worrying over her.

"Are you feeling okay, Mrs. Wheeler?"

"Just a little tired today."

Kellie narrowed her gaze. The woman looked healthy as a horse. She gave her landlady's arm a quick and awkward pat. "Okay then, sleep well."

"You, too."

Kelly headed up the back stairs to her room. She had her own bathroom and a makeshift kitchen set up with a dorm-sized refrigerator, hot plate and George Foreman grill. What more could a girl want?

A whole lot more.

In time, things would be where she wanted them to be. Right where she'd prepared for things to be. Years of putting herself through school with menial jobs and student loans lay behind her. A good future lay ahead.

If she got that job in Traverse City.

Kellie kicked off her boots, shrugged out of her jacket and scarf and settled on the lumpy futon couch situated between two long, thin windows that overlooked the driveway. She pulled out her phone and scanned the internet for Ryan's name and address. She found an R. Marsh with an address near her own.

3410 Lakeshore Drive.

No way did he live only a few houses away from her. In fact, they'd passed his place to get to hers. How could she have not noticed his address on his assessment paperwork? But then, he'd unnerved her from the beginning.

She jotted down his address onto an envelope. She'd confirm it at outpatient and then, as soon as she got paid from her part-time job, she'd drop fifty bucks into his mailbox.

Saturday morning, Ryan stepped into the office of Three Corner Community Church. His new sister-in-law had told him he'd find his brother here preparing for Sunday's sermon.

Sinclair looked up once he heard him coming down the short hallway. "Hey, Ryan, what's up?"

"Do you have a minute?" Ryan wasn't on easy terms with his brother. Not like they used to be.

Three years ago, Sinclair had dared Sara to mow an S in the grass growing on the side of a hill along the hayfield they were cutting. Sara's tractor flipped and crushed her. And Sinclair had run off on a mission trip to Haiti a week after the funeral. He'd stayed there until only a few months ago.

"Yeah, sure." His brother cocked his head to the side and waited.

Ryan sat down. He hadn't seen much of his brother since he'd recently married Sara's sister, Hope. Ryan was glad they'd finally gotten together, but watching them around the Marsh family dinner table reminded him too much of happier times. He didn't want to dampen their happiness with his dark moods, so he'd stayed away.

Ryan spotted Sinclair and Hope's wedding picture on the desk and his fists clenched. "I need to do some community service hours and wondered if you knew of a good place around here."

Sinclair sat forward. "Actually, I have the perfect solution.

A single mom in our congregation is having a house built by a nonprofit group of churches that builds homes for needy families. They could really use someone with your skills."

Ryan nodded. He'd been picking away at refurbishing his cottage for over a year now. Other than minor finishing work, it was pretty much done.

His brother pushed a sticky note with contact information toward him. "This is the church in charge of the program, and Jeff is the guy who oversees the construction."

"Thanks." Ryan picked it up and slipped the note in his wallet.

"So, how's it going?"

Ryan shrugged. "Not like I'd ever planned. Mom probably told you, but that agency I had to see recommended me for counseling. So, I'm stuck for the next couple of months."

Sinclair steepled his fingers. "Maybe it will help."

"Right." Ryan narrowed his gaze. "What did you tell that intern?"

His brother didn't look away. "I told her what happened to Sara. And I told her that we're all worried about you."

Ryan nodded. There were things about that day he didn't want to revisit. It was hard enough blocking out the vision of his fiancée lying on the ground. Another thing entirely to keep from hearing her last words spoken over and over in his dreams. The feel of her last kiss…

"Man, I'm sorry about all this." Sinclair covered Ryan's hand.

Ryan pulled back and stood. "Yeah, me, too. Thanks for the info. I'll check it out."

He made his way to the door.

"Ryan?"

He turned and looked at his brother's concerned face. "Yeah?"

"If you need anything, I'm here. I'll always be here."

"Thanks." Ryan nodded and left.

Sinclair hadn't been around after the funeral when he'd needed his brother the most. When his life had stretched empty before him, Ryan had faced it alone knowing no one really knew what it had been like. Only Sinclair had been there the day of the accident. Only Sinclair knew what he'd gone through watching Sara die.

It was too late for talking out those feelings now.

Three years too late.

Chapter Three

Ugh! Forty degrees and rainy and her car was in the shop. Kellie shivered but kept pedaling. Her breath billowed white before her, and she had to blink constantly to clear the raindrops from her eyes. She should have worn a ball cap instead of the knitted hat she had on underneath her rain slicker.

She'd only ridden a mile out of town and already her jeans were soaked. Four more to go in this miserable mess. As soon as she got paid next week, she'd repay Ryan Marsh for the tow truck. Her car would be done before that, but she'd have to use her credit card to pay for it. Another climb on that plastic balance didn't sit well, but she didn't have much of a choice.

A car passed by, splashing dirty water all over her feet. Kellie gritted her teeth as cold rain trickled down her neck, but she kept pedaling. She puffed another billow of white breath in the cold evening air and picked up the pace in order to make the hill in front of her.

The exertion warmed her, but not even halfway up the hill, Kellie couldn't push anymore. She slipped off her bike to walk the rest of the way when a dark blue pickup truck pulled off the road up ahead.

She knew that truck. And the tall man getting out of the driver's side. Ryan Marsh, bundled in a dark gray rain parka, shortened the distance between them in no time.

He reached for her bike with his big square hands. "Come on, I'll give you a ride."

Kellie didn't let go. "No need. I've got it."

The rain grew more insistent. So did Ryan's expression. "You really think I'm going to leave you out here? You're hard to see in this soup."

Kellie had reflectors on her bike and a reflective strip across her backpack and rain slicker, but as dusk grew closer, so did patches of fog and mist. She glanced at the cab of his truck promising dry warmth and a quicker ride home. Her hands were cold inside damp gloves.

"It's not like your place is out of my way. I live only a few houses down from you. Plus, I've got some questions about group sessions." Ryan shrugged deeper into the hood of his jacket while rain trickled down the front. "I could really use your insight into what to expect."

Kellie looked into his pleading eyes and felt the refusal die on her lips. He wanted her help. She wanted to get warm. How harmful could it be?

Kellie nodded and let go of her bike. She watched Ryan lift it with ease into the truck's bed. She slipped off her backpack, climbed into the passenger side and buckled up.

Ryan settled in behind the wheel bringing with him a spray of raindrops. He cranked up the heat and pointed to the cup holders in the flip-down console between them. "I just filled my travel mug with hot chocolate at the gas station. Help yourself."

Kellie looked with longing at the giant insulated mug, steam rising from the lid. She glanced in the backseat and spotted a brown grocery bag. What was in the bag? "No. That's okay."

He gave her quizzical look. "Kellie, go ahead and have it. You're frozen. And in case you're wondering what's in the bag back there, it's milk and cereal, not beer."

True, she'd been wondering and nodded. Cold shivers racked her body and she suddenly didn't care about drinking after him. Stripping off her wet gloves, she reached for the metal mug. She cradled her hands around the stainless steel warmth and sighed. "Thanks."

"No problem." Looking in his mirror, he pulled back out onto the road.

After a few sips of hot chocolate, Kellie got down to business. This couldn't be a social call. "You wanted insight into your sessions?"

"I don't understand what I'm supposed to do."

"You've met with John about your goals, right?"

"Yeah. My goal is to get this done and over with as quickly as possible."

Kellie shifted in her seat so she could better see Ryan's face. He looked annoyed. "Group will mean more if you focus on each session instead of the end result. Give yourself permission to open up and share your feelings in a safe environment."

He gave a rude snort. "I'm not comfortable talking about my feelings with people I know let alone to an entire group of strangers."

Kellie took another sip of chocolate. She didn't point out that his refusal to deal with his feelings was what got him to this point. Ryan probably felt too much, and being the hero-type he wouldn't dream of burdening someone else with his baggage. He'd carry his own, never wanting to appear weak or needy.

Kellie could definitely relate. Self-dependence was her mantra. Her safety measure. Maybe she didn't let herself feel enough because strong feelings needed an outlet for release. She shook off those thoughts. Counseling required a certain level of emotional distance, and she'd learned how to distance herself pretty well.

Another sip of hot chocolate and she felt more human and less like a wet sponge. "Vocalizing can minimize the power those feelings have."

He looked at her. "Talking about it isn't going to make it go away."

"How do you know?"

Ryan didn't answer.

Kellie figured that he'd probably never talked about how the death of his fiancée had affected him. How if affected him still. Bottling up that much emotion was bound to one day pop his cork. Was it any wonder he'd sought something to numb the pain?

Silence stretched inside his truck emphasizing the whish-whish from the windshield wipers and the gentle hum of the heater. Kellie noticed that they had pulled on to their road. They were coming up to what should be his mailbox, but one of the numbers was missing. She'd already checked.

As if reading her mind, Ryan pointed in confirmation. "I live right there. I go through town every day on my way to work, so I can give you a ride tomorrow if you need it."

"Thanks, but—"

He raised a hand. "I know, I know. Conflict of interest."

"Ethics." She smiled. "Accepting another ride from you is a definite conflict of ethics."

Ryan shook his head. "That's stupid. I suppose lying sprawled on the side of the road after you'd been clipped by a driver who couldn't see you is more noble."

He had a point. "I'm here, aren't I?"

"Yeah, you are."

He pulled into her driveway and stopped along a row

of trees. Putting the vehicle in Park and shutting off the noisy wipers, Ryan turned toward her with a grim face. "Look, I don't *want* to feel the way I do."

Listening to the sound of rain dancing along the roof of Ryan's truck, Kellie held back from asking the obvious question of how he felt. She had a pretty good idea but had no business trying to counsel this guy through his issues. They tread dangerous ground as it was considering the intimate setting inside his warm truck.

She glanced at the mug of hot chocolate she'd been drinking, and the temptation to do *something* for him tugged at her. She looked him square in the eye. "Give group an honest effort. You'll be surprised."

"I don't deserve this."

Kellie's hackles rose. That was a typical reaction from a person in denial. How many times had she heard someone say they didn't *deserve* court-ordered treatment because it was someone else's fault for the pickle they found themselves in? Disappointment swamped her. She'd thought maybe Ryan was different. Guess not.

She let loose a sigh. "No one forced you to go to that party."

His gaze bore into hers, dark and angry. "I don't deserve to be surprised, okay? Or happy."

Kellie blinked. Talk about self-punishment. Ryan had beaten himself up long enough and he needed more than her playing counselor right now. They shared the same faith and yet a pat word of encouragement would never be enough. Ryan needed truth spoken into his life, but even more so, the guy needed peace. She couldn't give him that. Only God could.

Searching her heart for the right words, she came up with the obvious. Or maybe God did. "No one deserves the gift of salvation, but Jesus died for us anyway so we'd have the right path to forgiveness."

Ryan turned and stared out of the windshield, past the rivulets of rain running down the glass, past even the driveway that led to a yard spanning the short distance to the lake. Lake Leelanau was shrouded in mist.

Kellie didn't know what he saw, but she'd guess that he revisited his fiancée's accident frequently. Her heart twisted.

Gently, she touched his arm. "Group might be the path you need to take in order to forgive yourself."

His hand covered hers. "I'll try."

"Good." Kellie gave his arm a quick squeeze and noticed the mass of hard strength below layers of jacket and shirt.

Time to leave.

She made a move toward the door but Ryan held fast to her hand, stalling her. "You're easy to talk to, did you know that?"

Considering the line of work she'd chosen, she hoped so. Considering the nice warm feel of Ryan's hand on her own, she needed to get out of there fast.

"Thanks." She pulled free and opened the passenger side door. A blast of damp cold air was exactly what she needed.

"Thanks for the ride and the hot chocolate. I can get my bike from here."

The last part fell on deaf ears. Ryan was already out of his vehicle. He hopped up into the long bed of his truck as if the high height were nothing and handed down her bike.

Kellie took it, careful not to look into the trap of his eyes. "Thanks again."

"See you around, Kellie."

She waved, still not looking at him. She hoped she didn't see Ryan around. In fact, she'd be much safer if she never saw him again.

The following week, while sitting in group listening to others share some frighteningly personal stuff, Ryan remembered his promise to Kellie. He'd try. He'd even prayed for patience through this whole group therapy thing. Bottom line, he couldn't go on like he had. Isolated in his grief, he needed something more than beer to get through the empty nights.

He'd started his required community service hours working on the house for a single mom in Sinclair's church. It helped. Now that he'd finished renovating his own place, he didn't like being home alone with little left to do and nothing but empty time on his hands. Time to think too much. Time to miss Sara.

He leaned forward and rested his elbows on his knees. Running his hands through his hair, he nearly groaned. He was tired of being alone.

"Ryan? You okay?" John Thompson directed the group's attention toward him after a silent pause between clients.

"Yeah." It came out gravelly and raw.

That was so not true. He felt like he was breaking into pieces. Pieces he couldn't glue back together. His stomach tightened and he suddenly felt like he might pass out. Sweat beaded across his forehead as his heart raced with the prompting to be honest. Come clean and be honest.

"No, I'm not."

"You want to talk about it." John leaned back in his chair, clipboard in hand, ready to take notes.

Ryan's throat threatened to close up on him. "Not really."

"We can wait. Take your time."

Fighting against the quaking going on inside of him only made it worse. His eyes filled with tears, but he vowed he'd choke before he cried. "I—ah…"

He felt a hand briefly touch his shoulder. The woman with the tattoos. Jess was her name, and he'd been blown away by the harsh story of her life. Humbled.

If she could do this, so could he. "I need help."

Kellie left the elementary school where she worked part-time as a teacher's aide in her niece's class. She slipped behind the wheel of her recently repaired but ancient car and smiled when it started right up.

The repair bill was not as steep as she expected. That had been a huge blessing. Someday, she'd buy a new car. If she got the school counselor job in Traverse City it might even be sooner than someday.

It took less than ten minutes to reach LightHouse Center across town. She'd left a book in her office that she needed to study for her looming certification test.

Kellie pulled into the parking lot and her stomach dropped like a stone thrown in water when she spotted Ryan's pickup. She'd forgotten that he had group on Tuesdays. One of the two days that Kellie did not intern.

She checked her watch. They might not be done for a bit yet, so the coast was clear if she moved quickly. If she grabbed her book and ran.

Slipping into the lobby, Kellie gave the receptionist a wave. Marci, on the phone, waved back. Kellie made her way down the hall and into her tiny office. The book she needed lay open on her desk, right where she'd left it.

Snatching it up, she cradled the weighty text against her chest and headed for the door of her office. The telltale sounds of a group session breaking up made her move faster, but she wasn't fast enough. Clients spilled out of the group session room down the hall and Ryan was one of them.

Too late. He noticed her and nodded.

One look at Ryan and Kellie couldn't make her feet move. He'd been through the emotional wringer if his messy hair and red eyes were any indication. Trapped by the troubled look in his dark gaze, she backed against the wall to let people by. He seemed like he might want to talk to her.

She was floored by how badly she wanted to talk to him.

"Hey." His voice sounded raw and scratchy.

"You okay?" It slipped out before Kellie could catch it.

He stepped closer to let others pass them, and she inhaled sharply. Ryan smelled warm and spicy and distinctly male.

He cleared his throat, but his voice remained low and soft. "Step one. I'm powerless against this grief."

Kellie almost reached out to touch him. Almost. She clutched her book tighter instead. "That's good."

He hadn't said alcohol, but then that wasn't the only issue. Kellie believed Ryan had tried to numb his pain instead of dealing with it. He'd finally admitted defeat, and that was the starting point toward healing. The first step in recovery. She felt proud. For him.

"Yeah. We'll see." Ryan's gaze dropped to her hands. "You've got your car back."

Kellie realized her keys dangled from her fingers. "Yep."

"No more riding in the rain." Was that disappointment she heard in his voice?

"No more riding in the rain." Kellie shook her head. No more rides needed from Ryan. Then she laughed. "I thank God for the good weather we had after that day."

He shifted his stance. "So, uh, would you be up for a cup of coffee somewhere?"

Kellie's stomach flipped. He wasn't really asking her out. Ryan wanted to process what he'd just gone through in group. He'd said she was easy to talk to. That's all it was. That's all it could be.

But that was enough to get her in trouble if she accepted. She shook her head. "I can't."

"Yeah, I know." He pulled a white envelope out of his pocket. "Look, I don't want this."

Her eyes widened in panic. It was the fifty bucks she'd put in his mailbox. "Don't even think about it," she hissed. "Don't you dare."

He cocked his head like she'd gone crazy.

Kellie glanced down the hallway toward the group session room. Folks still mingled. She looked the other way and spotted Ginny watching them. Her breathing hitched.

Great. Kellie inched away from the wall. "Okay then, nice to see you, Ryan."

His eyes narrowed, but then he nodded like he'd gotten the message. "You, too."

Kellie's heart beat madly in her ears as she watched Ryan walk away. She couldn't breathe right. Not yet. Not with Ginny coming toward her.

"Hey, Ginny."

The woman's eyebrows lifted. "What was that?"

Kellie ignored the question and raised the text in her arms. "I forgot my book."

"Come in a minute." Ginny nodded toward her office.

Kellie's stomach sank to the soles of her boots, but she followed her mentor. Ignoring the itchy feeling that skittered up her spine when Ginny closed the door, Kellie asked, "What's up?"

"Be careful there, Kellie. Be very careful."

Kellie couldn't play dumb. Her mentor would see right through it and think less of her for doing so. She rubbed her temples. "I know."

"So, what's the deal with you and this guy?"

"Nothing. He was telling me how group went for him tonight. That's all."

Kellie didn't dare admit to the rides Ryan had given her or that he'd asked her out for coffee. If Ginny blew her in to John, she could be fired. And that would be the end of her internship, and the chance for the Traverse City school counselor job.

"Keep it professional."

"Absolutely." Kellie breathed a little easier, but not much.

Ginny watched her too closely for comfort.

She knew.

Kellie had to get out of there fast before she admitted to the attraction she felt for Ryan. Ginny had that kind of influence on people. She got them to reveal their inner most feelings with one look, but Kellie was in no mood for confessions. "I gotta run. See you tomorrow."

"Remember what I said." Ginny used her motherly tone, the one that brooked no argument.

"I will. Thanks." Kellie stuffed her nervousness down deep with a roll of her shoulders and hightailed it out of there.

Was the draw she felt toward Ryan plain to see? If so, she had some work to do controlling her reactions.

Better yet, Kellie needed to stay far away from Ryan Marsh before she lost everything she'd worked hard for.

Chapter Four

Kellie leaned over her seven-year-old niece's desk to check her coloring project. "Nice job, Gracie."

Gracie, missing both front teeth, grinned up at her. "Thanks."

Kellie scanned the second grade classroom where she worked as a teacher's assistant. The bulletin board was filled with colorful leaves cut from red, yellow and orange construction paper. Leaves also hung from the ceiling, but they should have been scattered on the floor to be accurate. A few days of strong winds had tossed most of the outside leaves from the trees. Something about the cluttered creativity of elementary schools warmed Kellie's heart, not to mention that kids were naturally open and honest.

Beth Ryken, the teacher she assisted at LeNaro Elementary, stepped close and smiled. "You're pretty special to have your aunt help out in the classroom."

"Yup." Gracie nodded as she used a green crayon to make grass around her drawing of yet another small house with flowers growing in the front yard.

Kellie was fortunate to have nabbed this part-time position at the end of the summer. It was the perfect way to work near her related field and earn some money while she interned. She was sick of slinging pizzas into the wee hours of the night and smelling like burnt cheese when she got home.

Beth cocked her head toward her desk. "Kellie, can I talk with you a minute?"

"Sure." Kellie followed the tall blonde toward the back of the room. "What's up?"

"I got a call from the school in Traverse City. They're checking out your references, so that's got to be a good sign. I think you'll get a second interview."

Kellie fought the urge to chew her fingernails, a habit she'd beaten long ago, but the temptation still reared its ugly head. She wanted this chance so badly. "So, what'd you say?"

Beth grinned and tossed her long blond hair over her shoulder. The woman was gorgeous but didn't seem to know it. A rare combo. "Only that you're great with kids because you really listen to them. I'm going to miss having you in my class."

Kellie let loose a nervous laugh. Everything seemed to be coming together. Everything she'd worked so hard for. "I haven't gotten the job yet. Besides, I have to pass section fifty-one of the Michigan Test for Teacher Certification."

"You will."

"I hope so." Kellie had been studying. Hard.

Saturday, she'd finally take the monstrous thing and in the nick of time, too. She didn't want to leave anything to chance and miss this job opportunity. Traverse City was the perfect location—close enough for her to be near her nieces, yet far enough away from her folks, who still lived in Grand Rapids.

Funny. Growing up, she'd pined for her parents' time and undivided attention. As an adult, she visited them when she had to for holidays and birthdays. Sure, she loved them, but she'd stopped depending on her mom and dad a long time ago.

"I'm done." Gracie popped up out of her seat.

"Very good, Gracie. We'll collect your work when everyone's finished with theirs," Beth said.

Gracie slipped back into her seat. "Aunt Kellie, are you coming to the house tonight?"

"I'm going to try." Kellie hadn't been there the last couple of weeks because of studies for her upcoming test.

"She's really excited about their new home," Beth said. "I'm sure you've noticed that houses take center stage in every one of her drawings, her collages, everything."

"Oh, I've noticed." Poor kid equated a real house with stability. Not bad for a seven-year-old.

Gracie's mom, Dorrie, had applied for and been accepted by a nonprofit group of churches that built homes for needy families that qualified. Dorrie did everything she could to give Gracie and her older sister Hannah a sense of security despite their many moves, and this new home promised stability. Something they'd been missing along with the fact that they never saw their father—her brother, Karl.

A twinge of guilt knotted in Kellie's stomach. A few weeks ago, Dorrie had told her that many of the summertime volunteers for the Church Hammers group had dropped off, leaving her house behind schedule on construction. Kellie still hadn't picked up the pace in helping out. She'd been too busy studying, both for the upcoming certification exam and teen group dynamics for her internship at LightHouse Center.

The bell rang announcing the end of the school day and kids bounded for their coats. Beth's instructions to leave their projects on their desks fell on deaf ears. Some gathered theirs up only to dump them on their teacher's desk and then race for their in-class cubby lockers.

After helping with the raucous mass exodus of second graders, Kellie returned to the classroom to help Beth straighten up and grade papers. She had plenty of time to make it to the construction site, work for a bit and then head home to study.

Kellie finally scooped up her purse. "Hey, I gotta run."

"Yeah, I'm leaving, too. Thanks for your help. See you later in the week." Beth gave her a wave.

Once in her car, Kellie rolled her shoulders. A few hours at Dorrie's might do her some good. She could concentrate on manual labor for a change. No brain exercises, no worries.

Kellie drove out of town, past her road and headed north toward Dorrie's building site. Church Hammers built homes every other year for a needy family. This year, Dorrie and her nieces were that needy family. Needy, like her. Casualties left in the wake of her brother's neglect and drug use.

Kellie parked on the side of the road where there were already a few cars and pickup trucks. One of them looked disturbingly familiar and her gut clenched.

No way. Not here. There's dozens of dark blue trucks in Northern Michigan.

Shaking off images of the man who consumed her thoughts enough lately, Kellie gathered up her work gloves and walked along the gravel driveway.

The newly sided house was a pretty little ranch on a large lot at the beginning of a quiet cul-de-sac. This struggling housing development lay smack in the middle of cherry country so the views were beautiful, especially in May when the cherry trees were in blossom. The builder who'd donated the lot must have needed a tax break since several other lots still sported rusty For Sale signs. Real estate, especially new builds, moved super slowly these days. If at all.

Scanning the darkening horizon, Kellie wondered if they were in for more rain. Thankfully the volunteers worked primarily inside. The house had been roughed in with the plumbing and electrical wiring completed. Opening the side door, Kellie stepped into the unfinished kitchen. Zipping sounds of electric drills and the tap-tap of staple guns greeted her.

"Aunt Kellie!" Gracie tore around the corner and launched into her arms.

"Hey, Gracie." Kellie looked up as her older niece Hannah hobbled her way toward them.

"Hi, Aunt Kellie." Hannah's recovery from a mowing accident that cut her Achilles tendon this past summer was slow but sure. She wore an air cast to her knee.

"How's the leg?"

Hannah shrugged. "It's okay. I have to go to physical therapy when the cast comes off."

"Take it easy until then." Kellie tugged on one of Hannah's pigtails. How would Dorrie manage that? Kellie would help where she could. "Where's your mom?"

"In the living room. They're hanging insulation."

Kellie nodded and stepped forward holding Gracie's hand. But when she entered the living room, she sucked in a breath. Ryan, wearing a tool belt and looking too much like a permanent fixture, held a swath of pink insulation while Dorrie staple-gunned the sides in place.

"Mommy, Aunt Kellie's here," Gracie announced.

Kellie heard Dorrie's greeting, but her gaze was fixed on Ryan. It appeared as though she couldn't escape this guy.

He turned and smiled. "Hey, Kellie."

It was a devastatingly handsome smile. All traces of having gone through an emotional meltdown in group last week were gone. He looked healthy and strong. And good. Way too good.

Kellie felt like a deer blinded by headlights. "Hi."

Dorrie looked from her to Ryan. "You guys know each other?"

"Yeah." Again with the smile, like they shared a secret. "We've met."

Kellie found her tongue. "Right. Okay, put me to work, Dorrie."

"Ryan's your guy for directions." Dorrie stepped down from the short ladder and whipped off her gloves to wipe her forehead. "I do what he tells me."

Kellie's startled gaze locked back on Ryan.

"Might as well take a break. I've got to get more rolls of insulation from the trailer." Ryan tucked his gloves into the back pocket of his jeans.

Dorrie nodded and gathered her daughters close. "Come on girls, I've got a job for you two."

Kellie looked around. This was the last room to be insulated. A couple of men were working on laying the floor in the dining room. And a couple of women prepped the kitchen for the dinner that would be brought in by more volunteers. Not exactly a big group. More guilt washed through her.

Ryan stepped toward her. "So, *you're* Aunt Kellie. I never put the two together. I didn't think you had any family here."

"Just Dorrie and the girls." Kellie had moved here because of them. And because she could complete her master's at the regional location of Western Michigan University in Traverse City.

"Talk about a small world."

Way too small. "What are you doing here?"

"Help me get the insulation?" He nodded toward the door.

She gestured for him to lead the way. They walked in silence through the front door outside into the crisp autumn evening. A huge builder's trailer sat parked on the grass beside the driveway.

Ryan lifted the trailer door and jumped up to grab some kind of metal cart. "This is where I'm putting in my community service hours."

"Ah." Now it made sense that he didn't want to announce that in front of the other volunteers. "Does Dorrie know?"

He leaned against the wall of the trailer. "Yeah. I figured she should because of her kids. She also happens to go to my brother's church."

"How long have you been doing this?"

He shrugged. "A couple weeks. The builder that oversees the project signs off on my hours for the court."

But Dorrie made it sound like he was somehow in charge. Did he have experience in construction, too? "I thought you worked for a research center that grew cherries."

"And some other fruits, yeah. So?"

"You looked like you knew what you're doing in there."

He smiled. "It's not rocket science. I finished up my own home project this summer. I know my way around the basics."

"Oh." Like he knew engines. Ryan Marsh was a pretty handy guy.

Clearly, Dorrie needed his expertise, and Kellie couldn't argue with Ryan's choice of community service. But something swished deep inside her gut like an unpleasant stirring of her defenses. Would Dorrie depend on Ryan for more than his construction help?

Kellie wouldn't blame her if she did. The woman shouldered so much on her own, and Kellie knew Hannah's accident had taken a heavy toll. Still, Kellie didn't like where her brain had gone. She didn't like the thought of Dorrie and Ryan together. But Kellie had no claim on Ryan. She couldn't have.

"Before I forget." Ryan stepped down from the trailer to stand directly in front of her. "I won't take this."

Kellie stared at the white envelope containing her fifty bucks. *Not again.* She looked up at him. "I need to repay you."

"No, you don't."

"Yes. I do." Kellie tapped her chest. "For me, I do."

"Why can't you accept it?" He stepped even closer and his voice softened and coaxed. "Sometimes it's more important for a person to receive."

In her experience, receiving led to expectations that were eventually let down or crushed. But it was pretty hard to argue with him standing so close that she could smell his spicy scent that reminded her of a cedar forest. Hard to breathe normally, too, especially looking into those bittersweet eyes of his.

He leaned down and her heart beat madly. It might even hammer its way out of her chest if she weren't careful. He was so close she felt the warmth of his body that beckoned like a cozy fire. She'd almost leaned into him, but she froze when he stuffed that envelope into the front pocket of her jeans.

"Learn to receive, Kellie."

She batted his arm away and backed up. A wrench of awareness hit her like a strong wave of heated water, pleasant at first, but frightening as the undertow threatened to pull her out into dangerous depths.

Ryan looked a little shaken, too, like he was caught up in an internal struggle of his own.

Keep it professional. Ginny's advice screamed through her mind. Ha! The feelings running through her were a far cry from that.

Pulling it together, Kellie raised her chin. "Show me what needs to be taken inside."

"Ah, yeah." Ryan moved back and readjusted the ball cap he wore. "All these rolls of insulation can go in. They're big but not heavy."

Kellie nodded and slipped on her gloves. She quickly looked around. Church ladies were bringing in food, but none of them seemed to notice what had happened between her and Ryan.

What had happened? Kellie wasn't exactly sure as she got to work carrying the pink bundles inside. All she knew was that she didn't dare let it happen again.

Ryan kicked himself as he watched Kellie walk away. What in the world had gotten into him? He'd been a heartbeat away from tugging her close and laying a good one on her. He'd actually wanted to kiss her.

He stacked pink insulation bundles on the metal cart with a vengeance. His attraction to this woman didn't make any sense. For starters, Kellie thought he was an alcoholic. And she wasn't anything like Sara, who'd been bubbly and engaging. Always cheerful.

Kellie Cavanaugh seemed guarded and unlikely to trust him or anyone. Was that what drew him? Her vulnerability hinted at a painful past of her own. Renting a room pretty much spelled out her financial situation, but he didn't know that when he'd paid for her tow truck. Even then, he'd wanted to take care of her because she'd seemed so alone with no one to call.

Ryan stopped piling on the bundles and readjusted his cap. He'd been given the twelve steps from Alcoholics Anonymous at his last group session. He'd heard of them before, but those steps had meaning for him now. New meaning. Because Kellie had been right about giving group an honest effort. It might make a difference.

He wasn't there yet, but he wanted God to restore him back to sanity and away from the grief that ate at his insides. He wanted to move on. Did that mean he wanted to move on with Kellie, or were his male instincts kicking in?

He dragged the cart filled with insulation over the gravel driveway. Entering the living room, Ryan quickly tossed the bundles inside while everyone gathered into the kitchen.

"Ryan, dinner's here. Would you come in and bless the food?" Dorrie smiled.

"Sure." Ryan followed Dorrie into the kitchen.

She was an attractive woman, even though she looked nothing like Kellie. Nice, too. But he wasn't interested. He took off his ball cap and raked a hand through his hair. Since when had his thoughts started categorizing women as potential interests?

He spotted Kellie by the sink. Since he met her, that's when. She wouldn't look at him, but her cheeks were rosy-pink.

Ryan cleared his throat and tried to concentrate. He wasn't used to praying in front of people, but he'd give it a whirl. "Can we all bow our heads? Dear Lord, thank You for this food and the chance to be Your hands today. Amen."

Amid the chatter of folks filling their paper plates from a makeshift table comprised of plywood resting atop two sawhorses, Ryan hung back. He noticed that Kellie did, too. She still leaned against the sink.

He walked toward her, feeling like he owed her an apology. "Hey, I'm sorry about that."

Her eyes widened. Their color nearly matched the blue of her fleece shirt.

"I invaded your space," he explained.

"Umm…yeah, okay, thanks." Again her cheeks flushed, reminding him of how pretty she was. And delicate, like a newly opened cherry blossom.

Okay, now he was really losing it, but he smiled. "We're good?"

She laughed. "Yeah. We're good."

"No more with the envelope?"

Kellie looked down at her feet. She had thick eyelashes that fanned the tops of her cheeks. "I'll keep it."

"Good."

She looked at him with friendly irritation. "Get in line, will you?"

He chuckled. "Ladies, first."

She went ahead of him, taking only a couple of small spoonsful of casserole, a handful of chips and some veggies. Her plate didn't even make a decent snack.

When he finally had a plate full of food, he leaned against the wall. Better not to get close, but his gaze kept checking her out.

"Gracie, come sit with me and let Ryan have your chair," Dorrie said.

"I'm fine." Ryan noticed that Gracie sat right next to her aunt Kellie.

Aunt Kellie. He'd never have pictured the pretty intern as anyone's aunt. Kellie looked young and had way too much nervous energy. Was she always like that or did he make her uncomfortable? If it was him, then why'd he make her nervous?

"Sit down, Ryan." Dorrie gave him a direct order with a wink.

"Alrighty then." Ryan sat down and turned to Kellie. "Your sister always this bossy?"

"She's my sister-in-law. Ex, rather, but yes, she is," Kellie said with a hint of a smile.

Ryan must have looked confused because Dorrie leaned toward him and added softly, "I was married to Kellie's brother."

"Oh." Ryan wanted to ask more but noticed Gracie listening a little too intently. And Kellie picked at her food instead of eating it. There was definitely a story there. One that he suspected wasn't good dinnertime conversation.

By the time Kellie finished eating, Ryan had gone up for seconds. The guy could pack it away, but then there was a lot of him to fill. She got up to throw her paper plate away.

"You don't eat much, do you?" Ryan stood next to her, tossing his very empty plate in the trash.

"Sure I do." She couldn't quite choke down the tuna noodle casserole and threw most of it away.

"Ryan, do you want some cake? I helped make it." Gracie held out a piece.

Ryan took it with a smile. "You made this? How'd you know chocolate is my favorite?"

Gracie shrugged.

"Did a little bird tell you?"

Her little niece giggled. "No…"

Ryan made a big show of his first bite. "Wow, this is better than I make. And I make a pretty mean chocolate cake."

Gracie giggled again. "Want some cake, Aunt Kellie?"

"Yes, please." Kellie smiled and couldn't help but ask, "So you cook, too?"

"If I want to eat." Ryan shoveled in cake and tossed his plate. "Your niece is a good kid. They both are."

"Dorrie does a great job."

"I take it your brother's not around much?"

"He's not around at all." Kellie failed to keep the bitterness out of her voice.

"Hmm." Ryan looked puzzled, but gratefully he didn't ask more. Not with Gracie back with another piece of cake.

Kellie took the offered dessert. "Thanks, Gracie."

"C'mere." Gracie grabbed her hand. "I wanna show you something."

"Want me to hold your cake until you get back?" Ryan's mouth curved into a wicked grin.

"Not happening." Kellie found herself grinning back as she followed Gracie down the hall to the bedrooms.

"This one's mine."

Kellie took a bite of cake as she peeked into one of the two bedrooms. The room the girls would share. The framed walls had only been partially drywalled, and the flooring hadn't yet been installed. Carpet would be one of the last details after painting. The place was really coming together with quite a bit completed since the last time she'd been here.

No doubt thanks to Ryan.

Gracie sat on one of two window seats. "Ryan made these for us. Aren't they cool?"

"Very cool." And sweet, too. Kellie couldn't help the warm feeling that settled in her stomach, right next to Gracie's cake. Ryan seemed like one of the good guys, but was he, truly?

"Pretty neat, huh? Ryan made those out of scrap wood.

I told you he knew what he was doing." Dorrie stood in the doorway.

"Talented guy." Kellie moved Dorrie's purse over and sat down on one of the window seats. It felt sturdy. She could easily imagine a fluffy cushion with matching pillows. A perfect place to enjoy the view of the cherry orchard across the street.

"I think he's got his eye on you." Dorrie lowered her voice.

Kellie looked at Gracie, but the little girl was looking out of the window at the darkening sky with interest. "Dorrie—"

"I'm just saying."

"Yeah, well don't. There's no way."

"Why not?"

Kellie gave her a pointed look. Due to a client's privacy rights, she wasn't at liberty to discuss the obvious why-nots. Even if she could, Kellie wouldn't in front of Gracie. The kid was a motormouth.

"We better get to work." Dorrie gave her a knowing smile.

Kellie's skin prickled with unease. First Ginny, now Dorrie. This really had to stop.

She stood too quickly and accidentally tipped over Dorrie's purse, and the contents spilled out onto the floor. Bending down to pick things up, Kellie noticed a letter had fluttered out and lay open at her feet. The words *eviction notice* caught her attention. She scooped it up before Dorrie could intercept.

"Don't worry about that."

Kellie's gaze flew to hers. "Seriously? I thought you had until the spring to move."

"Gracie, go help your sister." Dorrie snatched the letter.

"Awww, Mom."

"Go on." After Gracie left, Dorrie explained. "The property sold and the new owners want to move the trailer off the land before the holidays. Before the snow gets too deep."

Kellie did the math. In two months, her nieces would be homeless. "Where are you going to go?"

"We'll figure it out."

Could they get this house done before Christmas? "Have you told the construction crew?"

Dorrie stooped down and gathered up the items from her purse. "It's not their problem."

Kellie didn't agree, but she understood how Dorrie worked because Kellie worked the same way. Neither of them relied on others very well. There was less chance for disappointment if they didn't depend on others.

"Come on. There's work to do."

Kellie followed Dorrie back into the living room to hang insulation. As the evening passed, Kellie racked her brain for solutions. Her parents could take the girls, but would Dorrie allow that? She wouldn't want Hannah and Gracie to miss school here. They'd be the new girls once again. And Hannah had physical therapy coming up as soon as that cast came off.

Would Mrs. Wheeler open her home? She had the room, but Kellie didn't think the elderly woman cared much for young kids.

By the time they'd cleaned up and the volunteers headed for their cars, Kellie knew she needed to talk to Ryan about Dorrie's situation. He'd know if they could finish construction before Dorrie's rented home was literally carted away.

She lagged behind waiting for Dorrie and the girls to leave. But of course, they stalled, and all of them walked out of the house together. Ryan locked the door behind them.

Her chances were slipping away.

"Thanks for your help, Ryan." Dorrie loaded her girls into their car. "Good night, Kellie. Thanks for coming tonight."

"You're welcome." Kellie watched Ryan head for the building trailer to lock it.

"Don't worry, I'm leaving." Dorrie wiggled her eyebrows and then climbed in her car.

"No, it's not—" The denial died on her lips. Maybe it'd be better to let Dorrie think what she wanted.

Kellie waved as they backed down the driveway, but her insides fluttered when she heard the crunching of gravel behind her. She turned to face Ryan.

He looked surprised to find her still there. "What's up?"

"Can I talk to you?"

He smiled. "Sure. Want to go somewhere?"

Kellie shook her head. "This will only take a minute."

"Okay."

Kellie blew out a breath that curled like white smoke in the cold night air. "How long before the house is ready for Dorrie to move into?"

Ryan shrugged. "Depends on the amount of help we get. Why?"

"Dorrie's been served with an eviction notice she won't tell anyone about. I stumbled upon it, so we have to keep this quiet. Can we get this place done before Christmas?"

Ryan shifted on his foot. "We're going to need more help."

Kellie nodded. After she took that test, she'd have more time. Besides, Dorrie needed her. "I can be here every night."

"We'll need more than you and me." His voice softened, stealing her equilibrium.

"What about your brother's church?" Kellie offered.

"What about it?"

"Can't we round up some more volunteers from there?"

A shadow crossed over Ryan's face. "I don't know."

"Don't you go there?"

"No."

Kellie twisted her mouth to resist the temptation to ask him why he didn't attend his brother's church. But that was a question for another time and place. Sinclair Marsh's congregation was the most logical place to rally troops, and she needed Ryan's help to do that. Dorrie went there, but knowing her, she'd never ask for help.

"Would you be willing to go?"

He grinned at her then. "I'll go if you do."

He'd thrown down a challenge. One Kellie had little choice in refusing. She could do this. For Dorrie's sake, she'd keep her distance and keep it professional. She had to.

Raising her chin, Kellie met Ryan's gaze without flinching. "You're on."

Chapter Five

Sunday morning, Kellie stepped into a small country church that looked like something she'd seen on a calendar. A quaint structure with white clapboard siding, the place was also pretty on the inside even without stained-glass windows. Decorated with pots of rust-colored mums and pumpkins, it looked like fall but smelled like home with warm scents of Sunday dinner teasing her nose.

Dorrie looked surprised. "What are you doing here?"

"I thought I'd check out your church." Kellie sniffed again. "What's with the smell of food?"

Dorrie smiled. "Today is potluck Sunday. Everyone brings a dish to pass. If you want to stay, there's always more than enough."

"We'll see." Kellie typically attended St. Mary's in Le-Naro because it was what she was used to. She'd grown up attending a traditional church.

"How'd the test go?" Dorrie asked.

Kellie shrugged, but she felt pretty good about how she'd completed her answers. "I'll find out in three weeks."

Dorrie smiled. "You'll do well, I just know it."

"I hope you're right." Kellie looked around as the excited hum of people talking while they trickled into their seats gave the place a cheerful atmosphere. "Where are the girls?"

"Helping Hope set up for children's church. Hope is the pastor's wife." Dorrie slipped into a cushioned pew toward the back.

"Ah." Ryan's sister-in-law, who happened to be the sister of his dead fiancée. She'd gathered that information during her phone conversation with Ryan's brother for the evaluation.

Kellie sat down next to Dorrie, near the aisle. Setting her purse on the floor, she noticed that hymnal books were placed in little shelves on the back of each pew. She picked one up and leafed through it, but only a few of the hymns were familiar. Were these the songs they sang here?

"Aunt Kellie!" Gracie rushed into the pew and gave her a whopping seven-year-old hug.

Kellie looked up in time to see Hannah hobble her way down the aisle followed by an attractive woman with short dark hair. The woman was lovely in a fresh out-of-doors way, but she glowed with more than good health and pretty skin. Happiness maybe?

"Hey, Aunt Kellie." Hannah made her way around them to sit on the other side of Dorrie.

The woman stopped at the end of their row. "Good morning, Dorrie." Then she held out her hand. "And welcome. I'm Hope Marsh."

"Nice to meet you." Kellie quickly stood and returned the handshake. Did Ryan's fiancée resemble this woman? Had Sara looked that pure? An envious pang clipped her insides.

Hope smiled, and then her face brightened even more. "Ryan!"

Kellie tamped down irritation that the mere mention of

the man's name sent her stomach to fluttering. She watched Ryan lean close and give his sister-in-law a quick hug.

"I'm really glad you're here. Sinclair will be, too," Hope said.

"It's past time I heard my brother preach." He turned toward Kellie with a fixed smile on his handsome face. He wasn't glad to be here. In fact, he looked tense. "Is there room with you?"

"Uh, yeah, sure." Kellie remained standing.

She wouldn't mind talking to Hope a little more. Kellie wanted to squelch the morbid curiosity she had about Ryan's dead fiancée. It couldn't be good to feel envious of someone no longer around.

Ryan slipped in behind her, brushing against her back as he did so before sitting down next to Grace.

Kellie didn't miss the interest in Hope's gaze or the confusion. It was obvious that Hope tried to connect the dots that might clear up why Ryan sat with her and Dorrie. Not so obvious if Hope thought it was a good thing for Ryan to have moved on after her sister.

Someone called out Hope's name, and she gave them a wave.

"Excuse me." Hope squeezed her arm. "Maybe we can chat more after service?"

"That'd be great." In that moment, Kellie's impression of Hope was stamped and sealed as a good woman. If Hope's sister had been half as warm and caring, it was no wonder Ryan couldn't let go of her memory.

"Good morning."

Kellie was gripped by another hand belonging to a little old lady with penciled in eyebrows. Stifling her amusement, Kellie managed a return greeting. "Good morning to you."

"You new? My name's Mrs. Larson, and I hope you can stay for potluck afterward. I made lasagna."

Kellie smiled. "Really?"

Mrs. Larson gave her a wink. "The key to good lasagna is to mix mozzarella cheese in with the ricotta."

"I'll remember that." Once she had a real kitchen, maybe she'd even try making it.

Mrs. Larson squeezed her hand and nodded toward Ryan. "This here your beau? I didn't see a ring?"

Kellie laughed. Her fingers were bare plus she kept her nails trimmed short to keep from chewing them. Not real pretty, but better than the alternative of swollen, red fingertips. "No. This is Ryan. He's a friend."

Ryan stood and leaned forward to shake Mrs. Larson's hand. "How do you do."

Kellie could feel the warmth of him standing close behind her. There wasn't much room between pews.

"Ryan what? You look familiar." Mrs. Larson wouldn't let go of Ryan's hand, so he remained standing in an awkward lean-forward position that kept his arm stretched across her back.

"Marsh. I'm your pastor's brother."

Mrs. Larson's eyes lit up, and she kept pumping Ryan's hand. "He's doing a wonderful job here. So glad you could come."

"Thank you. Okay, I better sit down now."

Kellie swallowed her laugh. The little old lady was a riot and wouldn't let go of Ryan's hand. His arm brushed her back again. Kellie was boxed in the pew between Mrs. Larson and the solid wall of Ryan's body behind her. There was nowhere for her to go. It was oddly comforting and unnerving having Ryan so close.

He finally managed to pull his hand free, giving them both space.

Mrs. Larson gave them a wink and then moved on to greet someone else.

When Ryan sat down, he asked, "What was that all about?"

"I don't know." Kellie noticed that he ran a hand through his hair. She sat down, too, but far enough away so that no part of her touched him. This itchy awareness that raged every time Ryan was near was getting old real fast.

She spotted a folded paper in Ryan's hand that looked like a church program. Reaching out, Kellie asked, "Can I look at that?"

"The bulletin? Sure." He handed it over. "You can have it."

"Thanks." Kellie scanned the bulletin. Church members were listed with their phone numbers and various things they did in the church. Prayer chain, children's church, volunteer chair—that's the person they needed to talk to.

She leaned toward Ryan and pointed to the name Judy Graves listed on the bulletin. "Do you know her?"

Ryan nodded.

"We should talk to her, too, don't you think?"

"Yeah, sure, whatever." Ryan wiped his hands along the top of his canvas-clad thighs. He didn't wear jeans today. In fact, he looked quite nice in a pair of khakis and a thick turtleneck sweater matching the chocolate color of his eyes—eyes laced with uneasiness.

"Something wrong?" Kellie asked. The tension in him hadn't eased. In fact, he seemed more agitated than when he first arrived.

"No." Ryan Marsh was a poor liar.

Kellie scanned the congregation in front of them, but she couldn't figure out what the issue might be. And then she spotted Hope talking to a middle-aged couple, who glanced in their direction.

Ryan gave them a stiff nod.

And it suddenly hit her who those two people might be. Hope's parents. And that made them Ryan's almost in-laws.

Ryan shifted again. When he'd made that deal with Kellie, he hadn't considered seeing the Petersens at church. Hadn't prepared for it either. The last time he'd talked to them was at Hope and Sinclair's wedding. But he'd kept that contact brief and the conversation short.

He scratched his forehead, feeling guilty. Moments ago he'd been contemplating Kellie's hair. This morning, she wore it pulled back into a thick cascade of curls that reached past her shoulders. While shaking that old lady's hand, he'd been sorely tempted to bury his nose in Kellie's loose ponytail and inhale. Seeing Sara's parents made him ashamed of his thoughts.

Technically, enough time had passed for him to date. His mother had told him that more than a few times over the last couple of years. But dating someone new only made him think more about Sara. He'd tried it a couple of times and found it wasn't worth the effort.

He glanced at Kellie.

She gave him an understanding smile, but there was no pity in her expression. No fawning, or let-me-make-it-better look in her eyes. Only straightforward compassion. He liked that about her. She wasn't a coddler.

What he didn't like was how easily she saw through him. She seemed to know when something bothered him, almost as if she'd read his mind. He took in the burnished color of her hair before leaning back against the pew with a grim smile. Good thing some thoughts were not on display.

By the end of the worship service, Ryan had relaxed. A little. Too often, he'd glance at Kellie singing her heart out next to him. Like when she stumbled through the tune.

She'd given him a shrug and a grin but kept on singing even though she hadn't mastered the melody. Practically every song they sang seemed new to her. Kellie's voice was low and slightly off-key, but he wouldn't soon forget it.

When they broke for greeting time, she looked to him. "Is that it?"

He chuckled. "No. We're taking a break to say hello before Sinclair gives the announcements and a sermon."

She looked around the congregation that had become noisy with chatter as people darted from pew to pew. "This sure is a talkative church."

"Where do you usually go?"

"St. Mary's."

"Ah. I guess this would seem less formal in comparison."

Kellie snorted. "It's definitely different. But nice."

"Morning, Ryan." His mother's eyes gleamed with interest. "Who's this?"

Ryan took a deep breath. He wasn't *seeing* Kellie. Although getting to know her on a more personal level appealed, their relationship wasn't anything like that. Nor could it be. "Mom, this is Kellie Cavanaugh. I believe you spoke to her on the phone regarding my assessment."

Kellie held out her hand. "Mrs. Marsh. So nice to meet you in person."

"It's Rose, remember? And you're much younger than I pictured. Prettier, too." His mother tipped her head.

Ryan knew that look. He could only imagine the ideas rolling around inside her brain.

Kellie's cheeks grew pink. "Thanks."

"How's he doing?" His mom wrapped her arm around his waist.

Kellie glanced at him with wide eyes.

He shrugged. "It's okay. She's my mom. You can tell her anything."

"I'm not his counselor, Mrs. Marsh. But even if I were, I'm not at liberty to discuss it. Privacy policy and all that." Kellie looked worried, like she might offend.

Ryan almost laughed. Kellie didn't know his mom. Rose Marsh didn't offend easily, but she'd let a person know real quick when she was.

His mom gave him a squeeze and smiled. "Well, you must be doing something right since he's here, in church."

Ryan rolled his eyes.

"Not really my idea," Kellie said.

His mom only grinned wider. "Even better. Ryan, why don't you come out to the farm for dinner tonight? You should see what Adam and Eva are doing to the space above the garage. They're working like dogs."

"Thanks, Mom, but—"

His mother leaned toward Kellie as if he hadn't spoken. "My daughter, Eva, and her fiancé are renovating our farmhouse to become a bed-and-breakfast. They hope to open in the spring. In fact, we'd love it if you'd come, too."

"Oh, thank you, but I've made other plans." Kellie smiled.

His mom looked from him to Kellie and then back to him in wonder.

"I'll be there, Mom." Ryan didn't want his mother to think he was Kellie's plan for later. He gave his mom a pointed look to get lost.

"Some other time then."

"Maybe." Kellie looked uncomfortable.

At least she hadn't used the *conflict of ethics* excuse. His mom might have blown that one to bits. Ryan almost wished she had. But as he watched his mother scoot away to visit with others, he made a mental note to explain things to her. As an intern, Kellie didn't need his mother stirring up trouble by pairing them up.

He felt a strong hand on his shoulder and knew he had one more parent to introduce. "Morning, Dad."

His father was already reaching his hand toward Kellie. "Miss?"

She took it with a smile. "Kellie, sir."

Ryan spotted Dorrie slipping back into the pew and motioned for her to come closer. He didn't want his parents to get the wrong idea about him being here with Kellie. "And do you know Kellie's sister-in-law, Dorrie?"

"We've met, yes. Morning, Dorrie." His father shook her hand.

"Bob." Dorrie smiled.

Ryan gestured toward the front of the church. "Sinclair's going to start."

His father gave him a nod but looked from Dorrie to Kellie with a puzzled expression before heading for his seat.

"Your parents are nice," Kellie whispered.

"They mean well."

"They love you to pieces."

Before he could ask why she'd said that, Sinclair took the podium and the congregation grew silent. After a short list of announcements, he asked everyone to take the hand of the one next to them and bow their heads for prayer.

Ryan hesitated, but Kellie grabbed his hand. Soft. Her skin felt soft and her hand small in his. He absently ran his thumb along the back of her hand. Yup, soft there, too.

His brother ended the prayer, but Ryan didn't want to let go of Kellie's hand. He had to of course, and glanced her way as she sat down. She looked pretty in a rust-colored sweater and corduroy pants that hugged her narrow hips.

She gripped her hands in her lap, making Ryan wonder if maybe Kellie hadn't wanted to let go of him either.

By the time Sinclair had finished his sermon about love, Ryan was blown away by the change in his brother. Changes he'd never taken the time to recognize since Sinclair had come home. So reckless in his youth, it was amazing how Sinclair had spoken from the pulpit with real maturity. And God's anointing, too. Ryan had never before believed in his brother's calling to preach. He still wouldn't have believed it had he not heard with his own ears.

He looked at Kellie. "What'd you think?"

If the dewiness in her eyes was any indication, she'd been touched by his brother's message, too. "It was good."

Ryan nodded. "Yeah, it was. Come on, I'll introduce you to him and then we can ask about rounding up volunteers."

Waiting for the center aisle to clear, Ryan thought about one of the passages that Sinclair had read during his message.

Romans 13:8—Pay all your debts except the debt of love for others—never finish paying that.

He'd stopped paying for a while. So wrapped up in his own grief, he sort of forgot about everyone else. Ryan stepped aside to let Kellie pass.

"Are you staying for the potluck?" Dorrie asked.

He shook his head. "Not today."

"I think I will," Kellie said.

"Great, see you downstairs." Dorrie smiled and headed for the lower level of church where dinner would be shared.

Ryan steered Kellie toward the front of the church where others swarmed around his brother. He couldn't handle a full-blown fellowship dinner in his brother's church filled with warmth and love and both sets of parents. Especially with Kellie sitting next to him. It'd feel too familiar, and too much like the past he'd shared with Sara.

Besides, he could only concentrate on paying one debt of love at a time. Right now, that debt was helping Dorrie get her house done in time for Christmas. But with each step toward the altar, Ryan's gut twisted. He missed the way his life had been.

Sick of the emptiness, Ryan silently prayed to the only one who could make it different. Make him different. *Help me come back, Lord. Bring me back.*

Kellie watched the brothers after introductions were made. They were so different and yet so much alike. Ryan was taller and much broader, too, but there was no mistaking Sinclair as the oldest. Something about the tone in his voice made her think that Sinclair had been looking out for Ryan his whole life.

Despite what Mrs. Marsh had said on the phone that day about her oldest son being the one who'd always tumbled into trouble growing up, Kellie knew a leader when she saw one. They'd come to the right place for help.

Sinclair fingered the paper with Dorrie's construction site address, looking thoughtful. "Yeah, we can get some volunteers for Dorrie. When?"

"This week, and every week until it's done. The only day there's no work is on Sundays. But she needs to move in before Christmas. So that may change as we get closer," Ryan said.

Sinclair looked surprised. "That's right around the corner."

Kellie spoke up. "The new owners of her rental want to move the mobile home off the property before the snow is too deep. She has no choice."

Sinclair shook his head. "I had no idea."

"That's Dorrie for you. She tries to figure everything

out by herself. I only found out by accident." Kellie shifted her purse strap higher up on her shoulder.

"Thanks for coming to me. We'll do what we can. Hope and I can help, too. Not that we're pros, but we've been making some updates to our house."

Ryan looked a little sheepish when he asked, "How's that going?"

Sinclair smiled. "Pretty good. I convinced Hope to wait on painting the outside until spring. But we've been fixing up the inside a little here and there."

Ryan shifted from foot to foot. "How's her mom and dad?"

Kellie again sensed the tension in Ryan. Like a coiled spring, that hero complex of his kept the guilt firmly in place over his fiancée's death. Facing her parents must be agony.

"They're doing great. Why don't you stay for dinner and see for yourself. They'd love to talk with you."

Ryan's brief expression of pain was quickly shuttered and covered up. "Not today. I've got stuff to do."

Sinclair glanced at her with a question in his eyes. Did he think she was the *stuff* Ryan mentioned?

"I'm staying," Kellie said. The only plan she'd made for the day was taking a quick nap before settling into studying her intern book on teen dynamics for group. She hadn't fibbed to Rose Marsh when she said she had plans later. "I've got to try Mrs. Larson's lasagna."

Sinclair laughed then. "Actually, you won't be disappointed. Come on, you can sit with me and Hope and fill us in on what Dorrie needs."

Kellie looked at Ryan. "I'll see you tomorrow night at the site."

"See you later, Kellie." He nodded, but his eyes looked heavy with memories and sadness.

She followed Sinclair toward a side stairway and glanced back as Ryan made his way out of the church doors.

"How's he doing?" Sinclair asked.

"I'm not his counselor, but…" Kellie chewed her bottom lip. Ministers understood privacy and anonymity. She could tell him a little bit, right? "Actually, he's giving group therapy an honest effort."

Sinclair stopped before the stairs. "He talks to you, doesn't he?"

Kellie thought about how Ryan had asked her for coffee and she'd shut him down because of ethical concerns. Namely an unbridled attraction to the man. "Yeah. A little."

"That's good." Sinclair's eyes softened when he spotted his wife, and he reached out his hand to her. "Hope and I pray for him daily."

Hope smiled at Kellie with a determined gleam in her eye. "You might be exactly what he needs."

Whoa! Kellie panicked, but warmth spread through her at the mention of being needed. She cleared her throat. "We're working together to get Dorrie's house completed. That's all. I give him insight into group because I'm an intern there and I facilitate a teen group, but I can't counsel him."

"Of course not." Sinclair looked like he understood.

Hope nodded, but the satisfied look in her eyes proved she hadn't meant providing Ryan with professional help. "So, Kellie, tell me about yourself."

Could the woman be more obvious? Kellie didn't blame Hope for being protective of Ryan. She was his family. And Ryan had a great support system in his family. All he had to do was let them in to help him. But sitting with Hope meant an interview of a totally personal kind. Kellie found she didn't mind a bit. There was something engaging about Hope. Something genuine, too.

"I'm interning for my master's in school counseling," Kellie answered.

Hope's eyes shone. "Awesome. My degree is in early childhood education. What age group do you want?"

"Middle school, hopefully." Kellie wanted to get in at the age where a kid could be deterred from the wrong path if needed. High school was tougher and might be too late. Although it hadn't been for her, it had for her brother, Karl. He'd already been lost to drugs by then.

They entered the lower level that was jam-packed with people and the wonderful smell of home cooking. Kellie's mouth watered.

Dorrie waved from the line forming near tables laden with delicious-looking food. She herded her girls forward.

Kellie waved back. She'd never been to a church potluck before. The church she'd grown up in had spaghetti dinners on occasion, and Friday night fish fries, but those had been put on by the church for its members. It wasn't all this sharing of dishes made by parishioners.

"So tell me," Sinclair started. "How much needs to be done at Dorrie's?"

Kellie shrugged. "Walls, flooring, cabinets and finishing work, but Ryan could explain it better. He's sort of in charge."

Hope cocked her head and then shared a look with her husband. "Really?"

"What?" Kellie wasn't sure of the significance.

Sinclair explained. "That's the real Ryan. He'd help anyone, anytime, anywhere. My mom said that he'd kept to himself after the accident. He'd spent a lot of time helping in my parents' orchard, and then when they sold that, he bought a broken-down cottage on the lake that he's been remodeling. Too much alone time to think."

Kellie understood being alone. Sometimes she felt safer that way, and other times it was like being adrift. What if Ryan didn't want to be alone? Looking around the room, Kellie took in what he'd probably grown up with—love and support. Had he attended dozens of these potlucks with his fiancée?

She spotted Ryan's parents laughing with another couple. They were nice people. Sinclair and his wife were, too. A nice family that appeared to be tight and caring. And yet, Ryan had drifted away from them all.

She remembered the poem Rose Marsh had referenced when they spoke on the phone. Kellie had looked it up online and printed it out. Fascinated, she'd studied it, but could only remember the first few lines. So simple and fierce.

I fled Him down the nights and down the days
I fled Him down the arches of the years
I fled Him down the labyrinthine ways of my own
mind, and
In the mist of tears
I hid from Him…

And appropriate. Kellie believed Ryan had fled his feelings and the Marsh family had given him space to do so. He was an adult after all, but a desperately hurting one. One with too much time to spend running down the labyrinth of his own mind. Like Ryan's brother had pointed out, Ryan had too much time to think and that had led to alcohol.

A shiver of disquiet shot down her spine. Kellie liked this church and its people, but was she getting sucked into something she might not be able to control? Coming here was about Dorrie and the girls. Getting them settled into their house before the holidays had to be her primary concern. But the more she knew about Ryan, the more she saw shades of herself.

Pain was pain, no matter where it came from. Kellie had come to terms with hers because of an astute counselor. She knew how to deal with her feelings. Okay, maybe avoidance of getting close to people wasn't the healthiest way to do it, but for Kellie, it worked.

Would Ryan come to terms with his? Kellie wanted to be part of his support system, but she shouldn't get too close. And not only for ethical reasons of where she interned.

Ryan had the kind of family she'd always wished for. Another draw toward the man. Kellie couldn't risk the heartache of rejection by getting romantically involved only to be eventually kicked aside once Ryan got to know her. Deep down, Kellie feared she wasn't loveable. She was high-strung and needy. A mess. What guy wanted that?

None that she'd known, and she wasn't going back to that place, ever again.

Chapter Six

The next day, Kellie stared at the computer screen in her office at LightHouse Center. It was almost quitting time, but moments ago she'd received a call for a second interview with the school in Traverse City. Things were definitely going as planned, and yet she teetered close to the edge of something scary.

A quick knock at her half-closed door brought her head up.

Ginny stood in the doorway. "Kellie, you okay?"

"The school called me for a second interview."

"That's wonderful." Ginny's smile died as she took a seat. "Why the long face?"

Kellie shrugged. It didn't feel right not to say anything about her friendship with Ryan, but could she risk telling Ginny? "Nerves, I guess."

Ginny's gaze narrowed. "You put too much pressure on yourself. When's the interview?"

"This Thursday at one." She'd have to leave the outpatient office early. "But I'll be back for teen group."

"Good. Did you let John know?"

"Not yet, but I will."

Ginny patted her hand as she stood. "Good for you, Kellie. You've worked hard for this and I hope you get the job."

"Thanks. I do, too."

Once Ginny left, Kellie inwardly cringed. She *had* worked hard. Too hard to be more excited about seeing Ryan later at Dorrie's than about her interview. Something was definitely out of whack.

Technically, she saw Ryan in a community setting. Her sister-in-law's house was the product of a nonprofit group. Kellie couldn't escape that, nor did she want to. Still, attending church with Ryan had really pushed the line. And Kellie wanted to return to that church where Ryan's brother pastored. She liked the way Sinclair delivered his message. She liked Hope, too. They'd invited her back.

Kellie got up from her desk and marched her way down the hall toward her boss's office. With a quick tap on John's open door, she stepped in and breathed deep the fresh air. Due to the unseasonal warmth today, John had his windows open.

"I got called back for a second interview."

Her boss looked over the rim of his glasses. "That's good news."

His lack of surprise made her wonder if he already knew. After all, the superintendent was his friend and neighbor. "Thanks for getting me in the door. I wouldn't have this opportunity without your recommendation."

"I wouldn't have done it if I didn't believe you'd be good there."

Kellie informed him of the time and date. "Got any tips?"

John laughed. "Just be yourself and let your passion show through."

Again, Kellie nodded but her conscience scratched like

sandpaper. Her mouth went dry and she took a deep breath. "There's something you should probably know."

John lifted one eyebrow. "Have a seat."

Kellie would rather stand, but knew it was best to follow directions. "You know that my sister-in-law is having a house built for her by the Church Hammers organization."

"A good cause."

"I help out as much as I can, and—" Kellie stopped to double check the small voice that had prompted her to confess. Yup, still there making her heart clamor and her palms sweat. "One of your clients also volunteers to meet his community service requirements."

"I see." John leaned back to cross his legs. "Shouldn't be an issue. You don't have anything to do with my groups."

Kellie swallowed. She really needed a drink of water. "No. But I did his court-ordered assessment for Ginny."

"Hmm."

Kellie clenched her fists at her sides and waited out her boss.

He narrowed his gaze. "That would be Ryan. Does he bother you?"

Kellie almost let loose a nervous laugh. Bother her? The question should be more like on what level. "He's got construction skills, so he's sort of in charge."

"You can't skip out on your obligation to your sister-in-law."

"No."

"And obviously Ryan's needed so it wouldn't be right to advise him to switch services."

"No." Kellie held her breath.

"Could be a real pickle, Kellie." His gaze pierced her. "But I trust that you will maintain a professional distance while you're here at LightHouse."

Could she? She had to. "Yes, sir."

John lifted his chin with a quick jerk signaling he was satisfied and the conversation was over.

"Thanks, John." Kellie resisted the urge to bolt from his office.

Before she made it out the door, John asked, "Kellie?"

She turned. "Yeah?"

"Thank you for telling me." His expression was hard to read.

"You're welcome."

Kellie's breathing returned to normal by the time she made it back to her office to grab her things. John was good at reading between the lines. And the lines between her and Ryan had grown pretty blurry. Would she regret telling her boss once he talked to Ginny? Ginny knew she was attracted to Ryan. Then what?

Lord, You pushed me to tell, so the rest is up to You.

She'd trust God's prompting on this one, but it was up to her to keep her feelings for Ryan firmly in check. She needed someone to hold her accountable because she didn't trust her heart. She avoided getting involved in relationships because her need for affection had led her astray before.

Ryan's interest had sparked a yearning she shouldn't have. Not now, not when he was going through his own issues and she still interned. By telling her boss the situation, she'd risked that internship. Exactly what she needed to stay in control.

Ryan arrived at Dorrie's construction site early, before anyone else. Good thing he had a key. Stepping inside, he looked around. There was so much yet to do. Could they get it done in time? A knock on the door brought him out of his thoughts. "It's open."

"Ryan?" The voice belonged to his brother.

"I'm in here."

Sinclair walked into the framed and insulated living room accompanied by two teenaged boys. After quick introductions, he said, "Hope sends her regrets. She's got a meeting in Traverse City about grant-writing. Put us to work."

Ryan rubbed his hands together. "Let's get tools and supplies from the trailer outside and we'll get started hanging drywall."

Ryan smiled as they traipsed across the gravel driveway to the construction trailer. Three more was better than none. He appreciated his brother's quick response to his request for help yesterday at church.

In no time, the four of them got to work while other volunteers arrived. Each time the door opened, Ryan expected to see Kellie. A kernel of disappointment popped each time she didn't show.

"Looking for someone?" Sinclair's eyebrows rose over the dark rim of his glasses.

Busted. Ryan shrugged.

"We like her."

He didn't want to talk about Kellie in the middle of hanging drywall with a couple of kids nearby, but he took the bait anyway. "Yeah?"

Sinclair nodded. "She sat with us during potluck. I couldn't get a word in between her and Hope."

"She could probably use a friend like Hope."

"Why's that?"

Again, Ryan shrugged. He didn't know why he'd said it. For all he knew, Kellie might have a ton of friends and a full social calendar. But he didn't think so. She seemed so alone, with no one to call that night her car broke down.

"Pastor Marsh!" Gracie ran into the room and threw her arms around the back of Sinclair's legs.

"Hey, Gracie." His brother laughed, but Ryan could tell Sinclair held the drywall burden tighter.

"Gracie! Get back, that's heavy." Dorrie scolded her daughter.

"Sorry." The seven-year-old stepped away.

Ryan turned his head as he held the drywall for one of the teenagers to drill into place. He felt his heart pump a little faster when he spotted Kellie standing in the doorway.

"Hey." His gaze held hers.

"Hello." She quickly looked away from him to Sinclair. "Yay, we have more help. Thanks for bringing reinforcements."

"You're welcome." His brother then introduced the teens.

"You guys are doing a great job." With that, Kellie followed Dorrie into the dining room to help lay flooring while Ryan and his crew continued with their dusty job.

By the time dinner rolled around, the church ladies who usually brought the food decided it was warm enough to grill hot dogs outside on the deck. The wonderful smell of grilled food made its way in through the open windows and Ryan's stomach growled. The teenagers wasted no time bolting out the kitchen's door.

Before joining the group in the backyard, Ryan surveyed the living room. Not bad. The drywall that hung in place needed taping, mud and then eventually preparation for paint. A couple of more rooms required drywall, but Ryan couldn't expect his brother to give up every night this week to finish it.

Sinclair clamped a hand on his shoulder. "Looks good."

"Yeah, it does."

"How often are you here?"

"Every night."

Sinclair's eyebrows rose.

"What have I got to go home to?" Ryan couldn't keep that edge of bitterness out of his voice.

His brother's shoulders slumped. "Come on, let's go eat."

Ryan stalled him, regretting what he'd said. "Thanks for coming tonight."

Sinclair nodded. "I'll be back. Hopefully, with more help."

Ryan looked into this brother's eyes. There was so much more to be said. They both carried a load of guilt, but Sinclair had lightened his since coming home. How?

"Look, Sin—"

"You guys coming? The hot dogs are going fast," Dorrie hollered from the kitchen.

"We'll be right there." Ryan should let it go. Now wasn't the time to finally talk about the accident and the last three years. Besides, Ryan didn't know where to begin or how to say what needed to be said.

Sinclair gave him a nod. "It's okay, man. I get it."

Ryan looked at his brother. "It's not okay."

"We'll work it out, but right now there are dogs to be had."

Ryan laughed and followed his brother out into the sunshine. Sinclair understood and for now, that's all Ryan needed.

Kellie entered LeNaro Elementary with a skip to her step. The weather had turned warm and sunny. She'd squeeze in a quick bike ride after school, before heading over to Dorrie's. The day was too beautiful to waste all of it indoors.

Sailing through the hallway toward the second-grade classroom, Kellie gave herself a mental pat on the back. She'd done well in keeping an appropriate distance from

Ryan last night while working on the house. They'd chatted comfortably at dinner, and that was pretty much it. No long-drawn-out looks or near-physical touches. She was back in control and that felt good.

"Morning, Kellie." Beth Ryken's smile was brighter than sunshine. "Perfect day for our field trip, isn't it?"

Kellie halted her steps. "Uh, field trip? Where to?"

"You forgot, didn't you?"

Kellie scrunched her nose as she recalled something about handing out permission slips weeks ago. "Sorry, I guess I did. Hayride, right?"

Beth shook her head. "The bus will be here shortly, so if you'll make sure every student has their jacket, that'd be great."

Kellie didn't bother to point out that they'd probably not need jackets today. It was already warm, and the weatherman promised the temperatures would climb to eighty degrees. Instead, she got to work organizing the noisy second graders into a straight line.

At least she'd get her wish to enjoy part of the day outside. October's final weather luxury before autumn slipped into winter didn't usually last long. Sometimes they'd get a whole week of the fickle warmth, sometimes only a couple of days. Either way, Kellie planned to enjoy it, even if that meant sharing a smelly hayride with two classrooms of kids.

Once loaded on the bus along with the other second-grade class and their teacher and two chaperoning moms, Kellie settled into a seat next to Gracie.

Gracie grinned up at her, missing both front teeth. "Do you like hayrides, Aunt Kellie?"

"Sure, I do."

Eons ago, her parents had taken her and her brother to a cider mill. Kellie had loved the bouncy wagon ride around the empty apple orchard, while Karl had acted bored. He'd been only twelve at the time, but he'd had an acid tongue. Her parents had ignored his sarcastic remarks, and even then Kellie had wondered why they let her brother get away with his bad behavior. Her parents had ignored them both too much. Family time had become one of those fewer and further between events, oftentimes squeezed in as if it were one more thing on her parents' to do list. Kellie despised being another duty.

The drive was lovely despite the bareness of the trees. A few hardwoods still blazed with patches of brilliant-colored leaves, but most of the fall foliage lay on the ground. When they finally pulled into a parking lot, Kellie frowned.

"What's the matter?" Beth asked.

Her stomach tightened as she read the sign of the horticulture research station. "They have hayrides here?"

Beth laughed. "We come every year in the fall because they're too busy in the spring. I happen to know the farm manager, and he's great with the kids."

Kellie nodded. Control slipped away with every hammer of her pulse. Ryan Marsh worked at a horticultural research center. Surely, this was the only one in Leelanau County. And Beth knew him.

While Beth gave the kids instructions to remain seated until after the bus had stopped, Kellie stared out the window. Like watching the proverbial train wreck, she couldn't look away from Ryan as he approached the bus. Tall and handsome as ever, he strode toward them with a pleasant smile.

Was there no escaping this man?

Gracie pulled on her sleeve. "Aunt Kellie, look, it's Ryan."

"I see that."

After the bus parked, kids stood and then inched their

way out. The excited noise of chatter numbed Kellie's brain as she watched teachers and chaperones corral the students forward until they trickled down the bus steps to pool into the parking lot like a line of ants swarming a picnic basket. Kellie waited for the end of the line. She'd been charged with the job of inspecting an empty bus to ensure no one had been left behind.

Peering out the window again, Kellie watched Gracie run straight to Ryan for a hug. What was it about the Marsh men that made Gracie so affectionate? First Sinclair, and now Ryan. Gracie seemed too needy for male attention. Gracie's only constant male influence in her life was her grandfather, Kellie's dad. Wasn't enough though as her nieces didn't visit that often. It hadn't been enough for Kellie, and she'd seen her father nearly every day, but only minutes some days.

Ryan scooped the girl up without hesitation or fanfare. Settling Gracie on his hip, he looked surprised when Kellie stepped off the bus. "What are you doing here?"

"I'm a teacher's aide twice a week for these classes."

He gave her a broad smile. "They're fortunate kids."

Before Kellie could still the cartwheels going on inside her stomach, Beth sidled over to them. "You two know each other?"

Kellie nodded.

"She did my assessment," Ryan said.

Kellie gave him a sharp look.

"Beth is a good friend of my sister's. She knows." Ryan set Gracie back on her feet.

"He works at our house," Gracie piped up with a proud grin.

"Wow. Small world." But Beth's gaze narrowed in on her.

Kellie ignored the uncomfortable feeling of being analyzed, but she didn't miss the spark of disappointment in

Beth's eyes. Was Beth interested in Ryan? Then again, who wouldn't be?

Kellie glanced at Ryan as he stepped back to address their group. "Way too small, sometimes."

Beth laughed. "Troublesome isn't he?"

"Yeah, he is."

Beth patted her arm. "Don't worry. He's one of the good ones. A definite keeper."

Kellie's gut lurched at the implication. "It's not like that."

Beth looked far from convinced.

"It can't be."

"Why?"

Kellie's reasons scattered like the leaves as she looked at Ryan. He stood near a huge tractor that had two long wagons attached with bench seats and bales of hay stacked in the corners for effect. Something about his open demeanor while talking to a group of kids made her excuses seem insignificant. He was a good man. A dependable man.

"My name's Ryan, and I'm your tour guide today. During the ride, we've got one important rule. Can anyone guess what it is?"

"I know, I know," several seven-year-olds chorused while they jumped up and down with raised hands.

Ryan picked one of the boys to answer.

"No hitting?"

Ryan chuckled. "That goes without saying. Good answer, but the *big rule* is that you must remain seated at all times with your hands and feet inside the wagon. Anyone stands up, we all come back. Everyone got that?"

Kellie noticed the kids' eyes widen as they agreed to the directions Ryan had given with a stern voice. She wondered if Ryan would actually follow through and cut the ride short if anyone stood. Her gut instinct told her he would. So far, he'd proved to be a man of his word.

"Everyone load up."

She leaned toward Beth. "So what's the plan here? Hayride then head back to school?"

"Oh no. This is a big deal. After the tractor ride through the orchard, we get a tour of the facility and end with pizza for lunch."

That meant they were here for a while. Kellie looked around as she waited for the kids to climb up into the wagon. Ryan stood nearby in case anyone needed help. The research station was situated on a small hill with an awesome view of Grand Traverse Bay's deep blue water. The orchards had lost their leaves, and the spindly branches stretched toward the sunshine in one last yawn before winter's hibernation.

When it came time for her to climb into the wagon, Ryan held out his hand. "Watch your step."

She took it, not wanting to chance a slip on the narrow wagon steps. "Thanks.

"You're welcome." Ryan gently squeezed her fingers before he let go.

Kellie found a seat at the end of the bench and caught Beth analyzing her again. "What?"

Beth shook her head but gave her a wide, overly innocent smile. One of those smiles that hinted at putting two and two together to come up with four. "Not a thing."

Kellie shrugged out of her windbreaker. Squished next to a warm kid who leaned against her, Kellie was glad she'd worn one of the few short-sleeved shirts she owned. Tying the sleeves of her jacket around her waist, she listened as Ryan started the tractor engine with a low growllike gurgle. Smoke billowed overhead carrying the faint smell of motor oil and gasoline. And then the wagon jerked forward and they were off.

"Welcome aboard. Remember to stay seated and keep your arms and legs inside the wagon." Ryan's voice boomed over a cheesy sound system as he spoke into the microphone of a headset he'd slipped on.

She watched him steer the humongous tractor with ease out of the parking lot toward the orchard with a clug, chug and purr sound of him shifting gears. The T-shirt he wore stretched taut across his back, and her appreciation for the warm weather hit a new level.

Kellie listened as Ryan explained each orchard they passed through at a snail's pace. Cherries were the main staple here—both sweet and tart varieties. Some other stone fruit trees, as Ryan called them, lay situated at the back of the fields. They passed quiet beehives and foul-smelling deer repellant sacks hanging in some sections. The kids loved those.

Kellie was amazed that Ryan managed all this. The grounds were extensive, but the orchards looked neat as a pin. Piles of brush had been collected into one large stack in an open field.

"That's for the research staff's big bonfire," Beth pointed out. "It's open to their families, too, and I've come out with Eva. It's pretty cool. If he asks, you should go."

"He won't." Kellie didn't bother to explain why. Even if he did, she couldn't accept. "So, you've known him a long time."

"Since high school."

Then Beth had probably known Ryan's fiancée. What had she been like? Before Kellie could even ask, the wagon pulled to a stop near the research facility. The kids climbed down, and again, Ryan was right there to help.

Beth jumped down unassisted, so Kellie did, too.

Ryan walked alongside her as they entered the station. "What'd you think of the orchards?"

"They're beautiful."

He gave her a satisfied smile. "If you think so now, wait until spring. I'll show you this place during the height of cherry blossom time. It's something to see."

She'd seen the surrounding areas in full bloom before but walking these paths alongside Ryan would be something special indeed. "And your family's cherry farm?"

He grinned then. "Even prettier."

She nodded, hoping for that chance.

He led their large group through the facility. They didn't enter the research room that reminded her of a high school chemistry classroom. Instead they lined the windowed wall and watched as pathologists and biologists did their thing inside. Ryan answered questions outside about what they were doing.

Kellie couldn't deny that Ryan knew his stuff. In fact, he took pride in the place like he owned it. As farm manager here, his footprint was everywhere.

By the time they gathered for lunch in the exhibit hall, Kellie was hot and thirsty and ready for the steaming pizza that had been delivered. Getting their large group seated and settled down with their choice of juice or bottled water was a challenge, but they managed as quickly as possible.

With the kids taken care of, Kellie chugged a bottle of water and then reached for a second.

"Aren't you going to eat?" Ryan had a pizza box in hand along with a couple of bottles of water.

"Thirst first."

"I've got plenty for both of us." Ryan tipped the box toward her. "Sit with me."

Kellie glanced at the kids, who were busy eating. Both

teachers and chaperones were, too, so she followed Ryan to the end of a table with a few empty chairs.

Slipping into a seat beside him, she took an offered slice from the box. "Thanks."

"So, how's this field trip rank?"

"Fun," she mumbled around a bite loaded with melting cheese that dripped onto her chin.

He handed her a napkin. "First time you've been here?"

She nodded, still chewing.

"During the cherry harvest, we open to the public on weekends for wagon rides through the ripe orchards, and this hall is filled with vendors who make cherry-related products. It's good PR."

"So that's why you sound like a professional tour guide." Kellie laughed.

"You liked that, huh?" He gave her a wink.

"I did, actually." Kellie wasn't into how things grew. She killed every plant she'd ever been given, but she appreciated the research that went on here. Even more, she could relate to the hard work Ryan put in. He managed the grounds and its equipment, kept track of projects and prepped the field for new ones. "You really made everything interesting."

He tipped his head before taking a drink of his water. "Thanks. I love what I do."

It showed. "Why didn't you take over your family's cherry farm?"

"Too much risk. Growing up, I watched my dad lose his crop one too many times. I can't control the weather."

"Wow, I'd never thought of farming in those terms before. I guess you're right."

Obviously, Ryan had some control issues of his own. He found a way to insulate his losses by his choice of career. Close to what he loved, but without the defeat of ownership.

"Okay, what did I say that has you thinking so hard?"

Her heart skipped a beat, but she looked into his eyes anyway. "You don't like to lose."

He searched her face, and his gaze softened. "You don't either, do you?"

"Nobody does." She'd lost too many times as a kid. Between the lack of her parents' attention, the loss of her brother's love and her own self-respect from going with guys who couldn't love her, Kellie learned the hard way the only one to rely on was God. And herself.

Ryan pushed the box toward her. "Want another slice?"

"Thanks." She reached for another piece of pizza and felt Ryan's fingertips brush the inside of her arm, across the thin scars there.

"Whoa, what happened?"

For a split second Kellie considered lying like she used to fib to her mom when she'd spotted the fresh scratches. Berry picking, the neighbor's cat, clearing brush from the backyard—Kellie had a bag full of excuses to hide her nasty little secret.

She left the slice where it was and bared her arm a little more. "When I was a teen, I used to cut."

Ryan's eyes widened. "*You* did that?"

She wanted to hang her head in shame at the shocked look on his face. Cutting was how she'd coped, how she'd dealt with the jumble of emotions she couldn't express or get rid of. "Yes, unfortunately."

Instead of changing the subject, Ryan's gaze softened along with his voice. "Why?"

Kellie picked at the piece of pizza. Explaining that would take far more time than they had for this lunch break. "It was how I dealt with pain."

"By inflicting more?"

"I was a kid then, but no different than you are now. Different methods seeking the same result. Deaden the pain, even if only for a while."

Ryan's expression grew grim with understanding. Real understanding. He didn't think she was freak. He grabbed another slice of pizza. "Crazy, what we allow ourselves to do, huh?"

"Yup." Would group therapy halt his craving to dampen pain with alcohol? She prayed so.

Ryan had so much to offer. As Beth had pointed out, he truly was one of the good ones. In fact, Ryan was proving to be more dependable than she'd ever given him credit for.

Chapter Seven

Ryan thought about what Kellie had said long after the second graders left. Group sessions were difficult for him on many levels, but mainly because he didn't like losing control of his emotions. After that first breakdown in group, he'd kept his ears open and his mouth shut.

Maybe that's why it was so hard to talk to his brother. The last three years, Ryan had tamped down his feelings pretty deep. Talking about it all now might be like cracking open a snake-in-a-can. His emotions could pop out and run wild and then what? Would he lose Sinclair's respect? Would he lose his own?

He scratched his head. How could a woman he barely knew know so much about who he was? She understood him. Maybe because she had darkness in her, too. That feeling of protectiveness for her washed over him. He didn't like knowing she'd had a painful past, one that had led her to a self-destructive habit. How'd she stop?

Ryan blew out his breath. Thinking about Kellie was becoming a habit for him. Seeing her visit the research station with a bunch of second graders made him smile. She seemed easy with kids and relaxed without a trace of her usual guardedness. Considering her own struggles, she'd picked a good field in counseling.

"Good job with the tour today." Liz stood in the doorway of his office.

"Thanks."

"See you tomorrow, Ryan."

"Yeah." He nodded, cleaned off his desk and grabbed his jacket. He had a long night of work yet ahead, but he didn't mind. Working on Dorrie's place kept him from his own empty house and brooding thoughts. Seeing Kellie was a bonus he looked forward to. Maybe a little too much.

When he pulled up to the house, he scanned the driveway for Kellie's car but it wasn't there. Only a few volunteers had arrived—a couple of older guys with physical limitations and a woman who couldn't do a whole lot. He'd find some project they could work on.

They were a small group even with Dorrie and Kellie. Way too small for the looming deadline of Dorrie's eviction. By December 1, Ryan wanted this house complete and ready for Dorrie and her girls to move into. Possible? He wasn't sure, but he'd get as much done as he could.

Ryan heard the kitchen door open and knew it was Kellie by the sound of her rapid footsteps. His body tensed as the air around him seemed to change. Charged with new energy, he waited until she came into view and felt his jaw slacken.

"Hey." She quickly buckled on one of the leather tool belts.

He wasn't sure if anyone could look more attractive and feminine than Kellie in an oversized pink T-shirt and jeans with a tool belt hanging about her slim hips.

He must have let his appreciation show because her cheeks flushed and she looked anywhere but at him. "Dorrie's going to be late. Hannah has a doctor's appointment."

"No problem."

"Light group." She opened another window letting in the warm autumn breeze.

It still felt too hot.

"What can I do?" she asked with that low voice of hers.

Ryan shifted his stance. "You think you can help me hang drywall?"

"I'll try."

He fished in a basket until he found a small pair of work gloves and then handed her a mask to cover her nose and mouth. "You're going to want to wear these. It's pretty dusty work."

"Okay." She slipped them on.

"Your eyes look blue today."

One of her eyebrows hitched toward her hairline.

"Your eyes change color. I notice." Ryan shrugged.

He noticed a lot about the pretty intern who'd complicated his life. Remembering the tiny scars that marred her smooth skin, he realized Kellie was a complicated woman in her own right. He never quite knew what she was thinking.

She looked a little flustered as she scanned the room.

"Okay, what do we do first?"

"See that stack of drywall? We'll carry each sheet. I'll hold it up while you drill it into place. Where there are outlets, we'll have to make adjustments before hanging. Make sense?"

She nodded as she loaded up a pouch on her tool belt with drywall screws.

They lifted the first sheet and Ryan was surprised at Kellie's strength. "You're not bad for a lightweight."

"I'm stronger than I look."

"You're not kidding." There had to be a deeper meaning behind her words. Kellie wasn't a woman to be trifled with.

That wasn't his intent. Ryan had never been one of those on-the-prowl guys. He'd always wanted a wife and a family. With Sara that dream had been a no-brainer. But now, he just wanted to get through the day.

He jockeyed the drywall into position and held it while Kellie stooped down to pick up the drill. Breathing in drywall dust, Ryan coughed before slipping his mask over his mouth. He watched as she climbed up the stepladder to drill in the first screw. "Nice job, that looks good."

"Thanks." She continued down the line to complete the side.

"If you drill in a few over here, I can let go."

Her eyes widened and she stepped closer. "Oh, sorry."

"No biggie." He enjoyed watching her work. The way she concentrated on a task. She wore a blue knit cap and as usual, her hair had been braided into a thick rope that swayed against her back. "Just so you know, your eyes are pretty when they're green, too."

She looked up and scowled. "Will you stop?"

Ryan grinned under his mask. He was only getting started. It'd been a long time since he'd wanted to flirt with anyone. And something about Kellie made him want to knock down that guarded reserve of hers.

Although they stood close, they didn't touch, but he could feel her warmth. There was a hum of awareness between them that felt stronger than before. The connection deeper than mere attraction. They understood each other. He held on to the drywall longer than needed so he could soak it all in. Soak her in.

She cleared her throat, either from dust or something else he wasn't sure. Maybe she was affected by that energy, too. "How was group?"

"Huh?" Like a splash of cold water, she'd reminded

him of their need for distance. No doubt, she'd done that on purpose.

She held up her gloved hand. "No. Wait. You don't have to answer that. I shouldn't have asked. It's none of my business."

"Whoa—we're friends, right?"

"Are we?" Her eyes searched his.

"I like to think so." He wouldn't mind being more but knew that probably wasn't wise. Not now, anyway. "I hope so. And group is fine. I'm listening really hard."

She drilled in another screw. "That's a good start."

He feigned horror. "You mean there's more?"

She shook her head at his nonsense. "There's application of what you hear."

"Just like church." He stepped back and surveyed their work. "Good enough. Let's grab another."

They carried the next sheet of drywall and positioned it in place.

"Speaking of church." Kellie bit her bottom lip as she drilled in the top screw. "Where do you usually go?"

"A church in LeNaro. Although I haven't exactly been a fixture there. Why?"

Kellie shrugged. "I wanted to go back to your brother's congregation and wondered if you would mind."

"I don't mind." He had enjoyed sitting in the pew next to her this past Sunday. He liked hearing her low voice sing songs with gusto.

"Do you not attend there because of your brother?" She drilled in another screw.

He tipped his head. "At first, maybe, but more so because that's where Sara's parents go."

Kellie looked through him. "Do you think they blame you for what happened?"

She didn't beat around the bush. Ryan knew that Sinclair

had told Kellie about the tractor accident, but how much did she know about that day? How much did she know about the strained relationship he had with his brother?

He shrugged. "I don't really know."

Her eyes widened. "Haven't you talked to them about it?"

"What's to say? Oh sorry, Mr. and Mrs. Petersen, I should have told your daughter not to cut that patch of grass on the hill."

Kellie stepped close to drill screws into his side of the drywall. "Would she have listened to you?"

He let out a sigh. He'd wrestled with that question for three years. "Sara was something of a thrill seeker, but she wasn't defiant. Growing up, she and Sinclair would try just about anything crazy. I don't know how many times Hope and I warned them not to do something and then ended up standing by to watch. We'd always laugh in the end. I had a bad feeling about the tractor stunt, but I didn't say anything. If I had—" His throat tightened up. "If only I had."

Kellie touched his arm, scattering white drywall dust on his skin. "You really should talk to them, Ryan. They go to your brother's church and he egged Sara on. If they don't blame Sinclair, surely they don't blame you."

"One of the twelve steps is making amends. Yeah, I know." He wasn't sure if he could complete that one.

"Are you following the steps then?" She let go to drill in the rest of the screws.

"Trying to." He watched her concentrate on her task. He'd never shared what he'd told her with anyone before. Not even in group. Something inside his chest loosened a little. Could she be right about Sara's parents?

"God will show you how if you let Him."

He knew that, too. In group they called it acknowledging his Higher Power. In his heart, Ryan knew he had to give God back His residency.

"What made you decide to go into counseling?"

She bit her lip. "It's a long story."

He chuckled. "Yeah, well, we've got a lot of drywall to hang."

She drilled in the last screw but didn't look at him right away as if weighing her answer. "My brother's a drug addict."

That made sense in explaining why Dorrie's kids didn't seem to know their father. Why no one talked about him either. "I'm sorry."

"Yeah, me, too." Kellie shrugged and headed for the pile of drywall across the room.

"Is that why you're interning at LightHouse? Do you hope to work there permanently?"

"No way." She snorted. "I want to know how to deal with addiction, but I don't want to surround myself with it. My master's is in school counseling."

"Like a guidance counselor?" He held the drywall in place.

"Exactly, but these days the position has been expanded to include more mental health and social aspects. I'm so close to finishing my master's, I can taste it."

"When are you done at LightHouse?" Maybe then he could ask her out and see what happened.

Kellie shrugged and drilled in the screws. "In about two weeks, I'll complete my internship and then find out if I passed my certification test when the scores are posted online. Until then, I'm not going anywhere. My boss John, who happens to be your counselor, has recommended me to the superintendent of a Traverse City school district."

"Sounds to me like you've worked too hard not to pass." Ryan gave her a wink.

"I hope so. One of their middle school counselors re-signed and I have a second interview for the position on Thursday."

Ryan watched Kellie rein in her excitement almost as if she were afraid to feel it. She caught herself, like she'd jinx it if she got her hopes up, if she showed how much this opportunity meant to her.

"What kind of duties will you have?"

Her face lit up again. "There's a lot of academic coaching, but also intervention if needed. Hopefully, I can catch kids before they head down the wrong road."

"Pretty tall order." The woman was on a personal crusade with her career choice.

She nodded. "It only takes one kid spared to be worth all the effort. A school counselor helped get me on the right track."

"How?"

She shrugged. "She noticed my arm and called me on it."

"And then what happened? Did you just stop?" Ryan watched her closely as she drilled in screws next to him.

"Not at first. I've got a few more scars, but I broke down and told her about my brother's issues, my parents' real estate business and all the things eating away at me."

Ryan put his hand on the drill. "What kind of things?"

She looked up. "I got lost in the cracks of my family and I looked for love and acceptance in the wrong places. A walking cliché maybe, but the hurts were very real."

"So how'd you stop cutting?" Had she stopped a bad habit to never pick it up again, just like that?

"My school counselor happened to be a Christian. She recommended a counselor for me to my parents. That counselor was also a Christian who helped out in a church youth group. I started going. When I realized how much

God loved me, I stopped marring His creation. We are His creation, you know."

Kellie might sound casual, but he knew better. Those had been painful years for her. Ryan had spent the last three years covering up how he felt. He hated the agony that pierced him every morning when he remembered why he woke up alone. Could God take that away? Could God make it all stop like He had for Kellie?

Kellie smoothed her skirt and took a deep breath before taking a seat outside the superintendent's office. This was her moment and she prayed she didn't blow it. Ryan said he'd pray for her, too.

The warm pleasure of knowing that Ryan would do as he promised, that he might even now be praying for her, morphed into trepidation. She was letting him in, letting him get too close. She'd never shared her story with a guy before, not that she'd dated much these last few years. Work and school remained her focus. But Ryan wasn't any guy. He felt like a true friend who understood instead of looking at her like some kind of freak.

If only her feelings could remain centered in friendship. The more she got to know Ryan, the more she wanted to know, the more her thoughts turned to what-ifs? What if they dated, what if they fell in love—

"Kellie Cavanaugh?" The superintendent and a woman waited before her.

How long had she been daydreaming? Kellie quickly stood and extended her hand. "Yes. Good afternoon."

"This is our principal, Maddie Grange. We thought we'd take a tour of the school first, so you can see how we run things."

Kellie forced a calm reaction even though her insides were doing cartwheels. "That'd be great."

Walking through the halls in one of the Traverse City middle schools was quite different than strolling through the little grade school in LeNaro. The kids were older, of course, but the school itself was larger and more modern, complete with high-tech computer labs. Was she ready for a professional job like this? Could she handle it?

She took a deep breath to calm her nerves. No matter how posh and intimidating this middle school might be, it was still a school that smelled like a school. That cross of scents ranging from pencil shavings, paper and damp coats to overcooked popcorn enveloped her like a reassuring hug. She could do this and, with God's help, she'd do it well. All she had to do was get the job.

"Where was Kellie tonight?" Sinclair grabbed the edge of the last couple of sheets of drywall.

The warm, summerlike weather held but wouldn't for long. Their weatherman had forecast the return of cold rain for the upcoming weekend. Ryan didn't hesitate in enlisting his brother's help to transfer the remaining stacks of drywall from the builder's trailer into Dorrie's house before they left for the night.

Setting down the last of the stack, Ryan straightened and stretched with a groan. "She has teen group session on Thursday nights."

Sinclair smiled. "You know her schedule pretty well."

Ryan shrugged. "Not quite, but I found out this week that Kellie is a teacher's aide for Beth Ryken's second-grade class on Tuesdays and Wednesdays."

"Why haven't you asked her out?"

Had his brother lost his marbles? Beth was like a second little sister. "Beth? No way."

Sinclair chuckled. "No. Kellie."

"I can't."

His brother's eyes softened. "Mom's right you know. It's been a long time since Sara."

It still felt like yesterday sometimes. "It's not that."

"So you've thought about it."

"Oh, I've thought about it." Ryan tossed his work gloves into the basket on the floor before facing his brother. "Dating Kellie could get her dismissed from her internship. Conflict of interest because I'm going through counseling there."

Sinclair nodded. "Oh. How's that going?"

"Pretty good." Ryan couldn't remember the last time he'd talked to his brother like this. Honest and open without the bitter anger.

Ryan had struggled with his brother taking off after Sara died. Sinclair hadn't even called while he was away.

Although, Ryan was having a hard time holding on to that. Times like these made him realize that it was good to have his brother back. And Sinclair had changed. For the better. He listened more.

Ryan cleared his throat. "Group is one of the toughest things I've ever done."

Sinclair's eyes were earnest, hopeful. "I know what you mean."

Ryan cocked his head. "How?"

"Coming back home was the hardest thing I've ever had to do. I had to face Hope. Her parents. You."

Ryan thought about his conversation with Kellie the other night. "Do the Petersens blame you?"

Sinclair shook his head. "No. They don't blame you either. Jim told me that Sara knew the risk of driving that tractor uphill and did it anyway. We both know it was her nature to do stuff like that."

Ryan swallowed the lump in his throat. "I could have stopped her."

Sinclair's expression was somber. "Maybe. Maybe not."

Ryan ran a hand through his hair. Sara might have laughed off his caution and done it anyway. She'd been driving tractors forever; she knew her limitations.

"Talk to them."

Ryan didn't want to talk to the Petersens. He'd let them down. "Come on. Let's get these windows closed and lock up. I'm beat."

After closing up Dorrie's house, Ryan said good-night to his brother and drove home with his windows down. The air was warm, balmy even. Ignoring the gnawing urge to swing by the mini-mart for a six-pack, Ryan pushed the gas pedal a little harder. He didn't want this craving, didn't want to accept it for what it might be.

It was a gorgeous night with a full yellow moon rising like a hot air balloon on the horizon. Pulling into his driveway, he stared at his dark, empty house and knew he didn't want to go in there. Not feeling like this. He hadn't left a light on. Didn't need to with the light that harvest moon was reflecting. He glanced toward where Kellie lived and knew what he needed to do.

Within minutes, Ryan silently slid his canoe into the still waters of Lake Leelanau. It was too beautiful a night not to come out here. And way too beautiful to be out here alone.

He paddled softly toward where Kellie lived and passed a group of mallard ducks that quacked furiously as they scurried away from him. That might be Kellie's same reaction, but it was worth a try. If not, he'd paddle alone and pray until he was tired enough to go home and fall into bed.

He made landfall and quietly pulled the canoe up onto Mrs. Wheeler's shoreline. The house looked dark from here, but he stepped with stealth toward the driveway. Soft light glowed from two upper level windows. Kellie's?

He spotted her slim, dark silhouette pacing across the room. Picking up a handful of small pebbles, he launched a few at one of the windows. Kellie stopped pacing.

He waited. Then he threw a few more.

The curtains were pushed aside and Kellie lifted the screen and leaned out. Her glorious hair hung loose around her shoulders. "Ryan, is that you?"

"Could you come down here?" He kept his voice as low and quiet as possible.

"Why? What's wrong?" Hers sounded worried. Alarmed.

"Nothing. Please, come down."

She closed the screen with a snap and then turned off all but one light in her room. In seconds, she met him on the blacktop driveway wearing cutoff shorts and a T-shirt, but no shoes. And she'd pulled all that hair back into a fat clip. "What's up?"

He battled a tenacious urge to toss that clip and pull her into his arms. Instead, without a word, he grabbed her hand and led her toward the lake, toward his canoe.

"Ryan?"

"Shh, just come on."

She stopped midway, pulling her hand back. "I'm not going anywhere unless you tell me what this is all about."

He stepped close. "Canoe with me."

Her eyes widened. Even with the brightness cast by that fat yellow moon, he couldn't tell what color they were. But they looked tempted, and maybe a little scared. "I don't think that's a good idea."

He was beginning to agree with her. "Look, I promise not to try anything."

Her eyes widened even more.

He'd given away one of his temptations. "I want to know how your interview went."

She folded her arms across her chest. "You could have called."

"I don't have your number."

She closed her eyes. "Ryan, we can't do this."

"Sure we can."

Her eyes flew back open. "Don't you get it?" She made a small measurement gesture with her forefinger and thumb. "I'm this close to graduating. This close to finishing my internship, and this close to a job I've trained forever for. Why would I blow all that?"

He stepped even closer. Afraid to admit to the other temptation he battled. Afraid to name it. "You won't, I promise. I need to relax and not think tonight. I can't go home. Not yet."

She took a step backward, but he read the recognition in her eyes. She knew what he battled against. Would she still go with him?

"Look, no one's going to know." He hated to beg, but he needed this. He needed her.

Kellie stared at him with big, round eyes.

He stared back. He wanted to kiss her but wouldn't. He'd made her a promise. One he intended to keep—at least for tonight. "Come on. You've got to see this moon."

He started for the canoe, then turned and looked back at her.

She shook her head but made a move forward. A sure sign that she'd given in. Most likely for his sake, but he didn't care as long as she went with him.

He smiled.

She scowled. "You say one word about this and I'll break every bone in your body."

He laughed. She was a mighty wisp. "I'd like to see you try."

She walked past him to the shoreline. Grabbing one

of the paddles out of the canoe, she gave him a warning wave. "Where do you want me?"

"Up front."

He turned the canoe so the front half lay in the lake and held it steady for Kellie to get situated on the front bench. Then he climbed in back and pushed off with one foot. He chuckled when she gripped the sides.

"Have you ever canoed?"

"A little. When I went to camp as a kid."

"Relax, we won't tip. This thing is as stable as they come."

She gave a derisive snort.

Ryan chuckled again. They'd already tipped toward something far more interesting than friends and he wasn't sorry a bit. For the first time in three years, he didn't want to shut down what he was feeling. He wanted to pursue it.

Chapter Eight

Kellie paddled gently and silently kicked herself for coming out here with Ryan. She'd been too keyed up over her interview to go to sleep, but that didn't mean this jaunt on the lake was a wise choice.

Staring up at the big, bright moon, Kellie commiserated with every woman who'd ever followed a man into trouble. She'd been stupid like that as a teenager; hadn't she learned anything? Knowing better but doing it anyway wasn't a good pattern. It didn't matter if nobody knew they were out here. Spending time alone with Ryan only made her wish for more. Made her wish for things she shouldn't want right now. Not from a man battling his own demons.

Guilt flushed through her. Tonight wasn't about her. It was about Ryan struggling against temptation, and he'd come to her for help. As a counselor, she'd already blown it by getting personally involved. But as a friend, she couldn't refuse.

"So, tell me about your interview," Ryan's deep voice rumbled softly from behind her.

She stopped paddling to take in the soft night sounds that surrounded them. "It went well."

"When will you hear?"

"Sometime next week, I hope." Around the same time she received her certification test scores. If she didn't pass that test, she could kiss this job opportunity goodbye. There was nothing she could do now but wait.

She stopped chewing the side of her thumb to dip her hand into the cool waters of Lake Leelanau and wiggle her fingers. "Can we talk about something else?"

He chuckled. "Nervous?"

"Excruciatingly so."

"You did your best, right?"

"Of course."

"It's in God's hands. He knows your future, trust Him with it."

Ryan was right, but Kellie wasn't the best at letting go and letting God. He'd never let her down, but then had she ever really trusted the Lord beyond her own abilities to make things happen?

Kellie slid around in her seat so she could face Ryan and the canoe listed to one side.

"Whoa. Tell me before you do that."

Even though she grabbed the sides of the canoe for balance, Kellie laughed. "Sorry."

He stopped paddling and tipped his dark head to one side. "What is it?"

"How do you trust God? I mean really trust enough to stop, I don't know, worrying?"

Ryan rested the wooden paddle across his jean clad knees and shrugged. "I think it's a conscious effort. A choice."

"You mean act like everything's okay?" Kellie wasn't sure she agreed with that approach.

Her parents had pretended everything was fine with their family when it wasn't. They'd ignored the warning signs from her brother until they'd been slapped in the face with his drug use after he'd been arrested. But her father had hired a lawyer and got the charges dropped. And her mother believed every excuse Kellie had dished out about cutting because it was easier than facing the truth. Neither parent wanted to examine the issues that lay underneath their kids' actions.

"No, no. That's like burying our heads in the sand. That's sort of missing the whole point. All I know is that I can't do this life well on my own. I'm figuring that out pretty quick, thanks to you."

"Me?"

"You saw through how I was trying to cope, and failing."

Warmth spread through her. She'd made the right call during that assessment and it had made a difference. "What if I got you a sponsor to call for times like tonight?"

"Not yet, but thanks." He shrugged. "I don't know about talking to a stranger, and wouldn't that raise a red flag for you to do that?"

Kellie nodded, hoping he wasn't deflecting her offer with an excuse. "I guess you're right."

"Being here with you helps more than you know. I've never really leaned on the Lord before. God has always been like a code of ethics I lived by, the dos and don'ts but not the air I breathe. Not that I'm there yet, but at least I'm seeking Him more."

Kellie briefly closed her eyes. It sounded like Ryan was making progress. That was good. It wasn't right to compare spiritual sidewalks, but she felt like he'd passed her in some ways. He tried to rely on God wholeheartedly. Did she truly seek God or keep Him in a pretty little package she only opened on occasion? When she really needed or wanted something like this job?

She sighed. "Thank you for sharing that."

"You're welcome."

"And thank you for your prayers about this job."

He pinned her with his gaze. "Maybe we should pray for each other. I sure could use yours."

Her heart flipped. She already prayed for him, but this mutual agreement to pray for each other sounded intimate, like something a couple would do. Should do.

She chewed her bottom lip, worried that this was one more step toward deepening their relationship. But then, no one should refuse prayer. "Okay. We can do that."

He smiled and then they fell into silence. Staring at the big yellow moon hanging in the sky, Kellie heard the sorrowful call of a loon that pierced the still night.

"Did you hear that? We don't get many loons on the lake."

"No?" Kellie imagined that the bird called out for a mate, so lonesome was the sound. How did it know if the right one came along?

"What's got you looking so sad?"

Kellie shook her head. No way would she admit to her loneliness, or her growing feelings toward Ryan. "What was your fiancée like?"

He looked surprised by her question, but thoughtful. "Sara was like a ray of sunshine. She made everything more fun, and everything she touched seemed golden. You would have liked her. Everyone did."

Kellie smiled. "How'd you two meet?"

"Youth group. Even though we went to the same high school, church was where we got to know each other. She was a couple of years younger than me but we clicked right away. Even then, I knew I'd marry her." A shadow of pain crossed his face but this time, he didn't hide it.

"High school sweethearts." Her heart pinched with

envy. What would it feel like to be the center of that kind of affection, that kind of real love?

He nodded. "Pretty much. What about you?"

"What about me?" She didn't want to get into her disastrous swim in the dating pool. She'd always given too much too quickly.

Ryan gave her a wry glance. "No boyfriends?"

Kellie snorted. "You really think I'd be out here with you if I had one of those?"

Ryan grinned. "You make it sound like a disease."

"Yeah, well for me, they are. I'm not about to catch any, that's for sure."

"Why not?"

Why, indeed. Because it hurt too much to be disappointed over and over. Because she hated waiting for her phone to ring. Because she wanted love too much and never got there.

Instead of answering, she shrugged and looked away.

"You're a beautiful woman, Kellie. Any guy would be beyond blessed to have you."

A shiver raced up her spine, but she wouldn't look at him. "Thanks, but I've dated enough who didn't agree."

"I'm glad." His voice was super soft and teasing. "Ups the chances for me."

Kellie looked at him then, and he gave her a wink. Her heart stopped beating for a moment. He couldn't be serious, could he? Ryan was still hung up on his dead fiancée. Maybe he only flirted with her to make her feel good. And she liked it far too much to let him get away with it. "Not if those chances are zero."

"Ouch."

She gave him a wide grin and he laughed.

Rubbing her arms, Kellie looked around. They were pretty far from shore. "It's getting late. We should head back."

"If you want to." Like a kid on the playground, Ryan didn't sound like he wanted to go in.

She didn't either, but knew they should. Scooping up her paddle, she gently turned around to face the front of the canoe. "I *have* to or I'll never get up in the morning."

Ryan started paddling. His strokes were long and even, propelling the canoe forward at a quick clip. "Maybe you should give me your number so I can give you a wake-up call."

"Maybe I shouldn't." She laughed.

Ryan's interest might be a sign that he was finally moving on. If so, good for him. But would it be good for her? Would *he* be good for her? That was something she couldn't answer. Not yet.

Monday evening, Kellie climbed into her car and clicked up the heat. Rubbing her hands together, she conceded that Indian summer was definitely over. She also had to admit she was rushing out of LightHouse Center more because she wanted to see Ryan than to help Dorrie. She flipped down the visor and checked her image in the mirror. A little lip gloss wouldn't hurt.

Ever since canoeing late Thursday night, Ryan had been nothing but friendly on the work site. They had both worked Friday night and put in a long day on Saturday to finish hanging the drywall. Ryan's brother had shown up with a handful of men, so the work had gone quickly.

Not once had Ryan flirted with her. She'd been grateful but had experienced a bout of disappointment, too. Still, they'd talked about themselves nonstop while finishing up the drywall. Kellie told him how much she loved bike-riding, especially on off-the-beaten-path kind of trails. And Ryan had confessed to a recent interest in fishing since moving to the lake. They had joked around but steered clear of any hints of a relationship. No promises or wishes. Nothing serious.

It had been great. Easy. And yet whenever anyone mentioned the regrettable end to their summerlike weather, they'd exchange a look. Paddling a canoe on the lake by the light of that big ol' harvest moon was a secret they shared. One she cherished. One Kellie hoped Ryan did, too.

She'd kept up her end of their prayer pact, even though praying for Ryan wasn't easy. Kellie prayed for Ryan's continued healing, but she worried that God might ignore her selfish prayers. Her motivation in saying them was more for her sake than Ryan's. She prayed that God would make Ryan into a man she could believe in. A man she could trust.

When she finally stepped into Dorrie's house, she was nearly toppled over by Gracie's bear hug.

"Aunt Kellie!"

"About time you got here, slacker." Ryan grinned.

Kellie laughed off his comment as she returned her younger niece's embrace. "What's the work duty today, crew chief?"

"Finishing the drywall edges with corner bead and then taping the seams. You shouldn't get too dirty."

Kellie looked down at Gracie's chalky white nose. "What have you been doing, miss?"

"Wiping walls like Ryan said."

Kellie glanced at Ryan.

He shrugged. "Something to keep her busy."

"Good call."

Lately, her nieces asked for stuff to do from Ryan instead of Dorrie. He told them his tasks were jobs he couldn't trust to just anyone, and that made the girls feel important. One more reason for her heart to swell toward the man.

Beth had told her that Ryan was one of the good ones. Kellie believed her, but good ones still fell. When would that happen with Ryan? If the other night's struggle was any indication, Ryan had given up drinking. But was it for good?

Working alongside him, they attached the corner bead and then screwed it in place. It wasn't hard work, not like the drywall that was heavy and awkward, and needed to be adjusted and cut for outlets. They moved along at a good pace. Cutting a piece of metal corner bead, Kellie reached across the stand to lay down the tin snips. She wasn't paying attention, nor wearing her gloves.

"Ahhhh." She pulled her hand back too late. The slice was quick and sharp, but she couldn't tell how deep because blood pooled in her palm.

"Let me see." Ryan reached for her hand.

She did what he asked but closed her eyes. Blood wasn't something she took well. She felt the light scrape of him wiping her palm with a paper towel.

He muttered under his breath.

Kellie opened her eyes. "What was that?"

He gave her a crooked smile. "I left the first aid kit in the trailer outside. Can you walk with me?"

"I hurt my hand, not my legs. Of course, I can walk."

He chuckled, pressed the paper towel into her palm and curled her fingers around it, keeping it in place. "You look a little green."

"That's because this is gross."

"Good thing you didn't go into medicine. I don't think you need stitches, but it still needs to be cleaned. Come with me." He grabbed a bottle of water, told a group working in the dining room where they were going and then headed outside.

She followed him to the builder's trailer with its roll top door left open because it wasn't raining today. The sky was overcast, and the cold air carried with it a damp chill. Kellie shivered. She hadn't thought to grab her jacket.

She climbed up the metal steps and went inside. It was a pretty small space considering that it housed tools and building materials. Shelves covered both sides from the floor to ceiling.

Ryan flipped on the overhead light that ran off the generator they used for electricity. "Have a seat."

She hopped onto a stool while Ryan located the first aid kit and a roll of paper towels. When he had those, he pulled another stool very close—right in front of her.

He looked into her eyes. "You want to pull that off or do you want me to?"

She offered him her hand, palm up. The paper towel she gripped had turned red. "You do it."

Gently, he cupped her hand with his own and eased off the makeshift bandage. It stung and she shivered again— from the cold or the feel of Ryan's fingers on her skin, she wasn't sure.

"You okay?"

She scrunched her nose as she looked at her cut hand cradled in his. The bleeding had slowed down. She shivered again.

"Hang on." He stood up and stripped off his flannel shirt and then draped it around her shoulders. The fabric carried his warmth along with his woodsy scent.

She clutched the shirt closer with her good hand and breathed deep. "Thanks."

He still wore a long-sleeved thermal shirt that clung

to his chest and arms, showing off the breadth of his shoulders.

Wow.

He caught her gawking and gave her a lopsided smile. His cheeks actually flushed a little.

Kellie looked away. "What now?"

"Hold this under your hand." He scrunched up a bunch of paper towels and poured water over her hand to rinse the cut. Blotting it dry, he examined her palm.

"Well?"

"You'll live."

"Good guesswork, Sherlock. Will a Band-Aid suffice so I can get back to work in there?"

He clicked his tongue. "No. It needs to be wrapped. And you should probably get it checked out and maybe get a tetanus shot, too. You sliced it on metal."

She looked into his serious face. He wasn't kidding. He was worried about her and that felt…nice. She watched the muscles in his arms tighten as he opened a little brown bottle of hydrogen peroxide. She managed to answer, but it came out a rough whisper. "I'll be fine."

"I hope so. This is going to sting."

Kellie nodded for him to go ahead and douse her palm. Boy, oh, boy was he right. She nearly jumped off the stool but watched his every move instead.

He gave her hand a quick squeeze, as he again blotted it dry. Then he let go in order to drizzle triple antibiotic cream onto a rectangular piece of gauze. Placing that on her palm, he wrapped it with more gauze and then taped it secure.

It seemed like forever and then he was done in an instant. She flexed her hand. "Feels good. I should be able to fit my glove over it, no problem."

"I don't know. You put pressure on it and it's likely to start bleeding again. Maybe you should call it a night."

She glanced down, noticing again how close they were. Ryan's knees protectively straddled her own. She looked up and whispered, "Thank you for taking care of this. No way could I have done it."

He brushed a curl back from her face. "You're welcome."

Awareness radiated between them and Kellie swallowed hard. Ryan leaned forward and grazed his lips against hers with the lightest touch. Then he jerked his head back and looked at her again with eyes that searched hers.

Kellie's toes curled inside her bulky work boots. Was he asking permission, giving her a chance to tell him no or what? Her heart pounded but the rest of her might as well have been paralyzed. She couldn't move, she couldn't breathe and she certainly couldn't form the words to tell Ryan to back off.

Ryan gave her a sly little smile before moving in close. This time, he kissed her with thorough purpose. He kissed deeply but with such tenderness, she wanted to cry.

Only their mouths anchored them together, but their souls had somehow linked, too, and Kellie couldn't think.

There was only him. There was only her.

She shuddered, and Ryan's arms came around her, pulling her close.

"It's okay, Kel," he murmured against her lips. "Let it happen."

Kellie pulled back as memories flooded her brain. The only other person who'd called her Kel was her brother, Karl. He'd let her down and stopped loving her. Her brother had cared more about his next high than his little sister.

Ryan let go when he felt Kellie push away. His pulse still thundered in his ears. His heart raced. And his mind twisted with concern. He wasn't sorry for kissing Kellie, not one bit. But looking into her remorse-filled eyes, he knew she wasn't happy with what had just happened between them. They'd crossed the line.

"Before you say anything, I know I shouldn't have done that."

Kellie closed her eyes and shook her head. "No, it's okay. It's my fault."

"How's it your fault?" He couldn't believe his ears.

"I let it happen." She spun on the stool away from him and hopped off.

Without a word, Kellie walked to the open trailer door and peered out into the dusky evening. Her shoulders slumped and she wrapped her arms around her middle, looking small and cold.

"Kellie…" He heard car doors slam and the crunch of feet on gravel along with feminine laughter. The church ladies had brought dinner. "Did anyone see us?"

"I don't think so."

He stepped close and stood behind her. "I meant that kiss."

"Don't." Her voice was low and scratchy-sounding.

If only he knew what she was feeling. He knew what he felt. Something he hadn't experienced in a long time. Not since Sara. He touched her shoulder. "But I care about you."

"Not now you can't."

"Come on, you're almost done at LightHouse Center."

She turned on him. "But you're not. And that's a problem. A big problem, don't you see?"

He didn't. She'd called it a conflict of interest. No, ethics. But she wasn't his counselor, so what was the big deal? He wasn't about to let her go but knew better than to push. He had some soul-searching of his own to do. Was he ready for this?

He gave her a stiff nod. "So, we'll wait."

She narrowed her gaze, looking like she wanted to say more, but the sounds of someone walking toward them stopped her.

Even in the uneven light shed from the trailer's single lightbulb, Ryan saw the color drain from Kellie's face. Maybe she'd lost more blood than he thought. He reached out a hand to steady her, but she jumped down off the platform and walked toward the man approaching them. A man he'd never seen before.

Ryan felt the hairs on his neck rise with an eerie tingle. Who was this guy, and had he seen them inside that trailer?

"Hi, Kel," the man said.

Ryan stepped off the trailer and moved toward them. Something didn't feel right, and he clenched his fists, ready to take the guy down if he so much as laid a finger on Kellie.

"What are you doing here?" Kellie's voice was barely above a whisper.

"Mom and Dad told me about the house for Dorrie. They said where I could find you. I want to see my kids."

Ryan's mouth dropped open. This slick guy with the I'm-all-that stance was her brother, the drug addict?

"I don't think that's a good idea," Kellie said.

Ryan stood next to her and fought the urge to wrap his arm around her. She still had on his shirt and clutched it close. "Hey."

"Ryan, this is my brother, Karl."

Karl reached out a hand. "Ryan."

They looked alike up close, although Karl was taller and appeared way older than his sister, but was it more years or experience that distinguished him? Even though his crisp jeans and fine knit sweater looked expensive, the guy seemed downtrodden. Defeated even. Considering what Ryan had learned in group, he shouldn't hold that against Karl, but he did. Because he'd hurt Kellie.

Ryan finally shook the guy's hand but with a little show of strength. "Karl. What's up?"

Karl looked from Kellie to him and then back again.

Kellie wasn't explaining anything. "You can't just show up and expect Dorrie to welcome you. Why didn't you call?"

Her brother shrugged. "I thought if you saw me, maybe you'd plead my case."

"Not here, and not tonight. You should come home with me, now."

Karl glanced at him, looking for support.

Ryan wasn't giving it. He squared his shoulders, ready for anything the guy might do. "You better go with your sister. Without her say so, you aren't getting near Dorrie or her girls."

Karl's face flushed red with rage. "They're my kids!"

Ryan kept his mouth shut and his gaze strong. He was too close to pointing out that Karl should have thought of that before he left them to fend for themselves.

Karl made a move toward him.

Kellie stepped between them. "Karl, don't make a scene. Let's go."

"Fine." Karl stalked off toward his car—a nice Lexus sedan that didn't look old.

Whatever the guy did for a living, it couldn't be that bad. A strong urge to pound the guy hit him as he recalled how Dorrie struggled financially. Nice. Real nice.

Kellie turned toward him. "Let me tell Dorrie my own way, okay? Don't say anything about this."

"I'll go with you." Ryan didn't like Kellie leaving alone,

but the guy was her brother. He wouldn't do anything crazy, would he?

Kelly shook her head. "You're needed here."

"But—"

She laid her hand on his arm. "Don't worry, I'll be fine."

Ryan nodded and headed back to the house after he watched her car pull out on to the road followed by her brother's fancy sedan. He prayed for Kellie ever since her job interview and tonight would be no different, other than this urgency for God to protect her.

Once inside, everyone gathered around the card tables set up in the kitchen and filled their plates with food.

"Where's Kellie?" Dorrie asked.

"She went home. She shouldn't use that cut hand."

Dorrie looked at him closely. "Is she okay?"

He ran a hand through his hair, hoping it hadn't been messed up by Kellie's fingers. "Yeah, yeah. She'll be fine."

Dorrie's gaze narrowed even more and then she smiled. "So, where's your shirt?"

He tried his best to sound casual. "Kellie's got it. She was chilled."

"Mmm-hmm."

"Smells good in here. What have we got tonight?" Ryan addressed one of the church ladies. He knew the only way out of this one was changing the subject fast, as well as not looking Dorrie in the eye.

As he listened to the elderly lady list off every dish that had been brought, Ryan worried about Kellie. He couldn't ask Dorrie about Karl, not here. Not in front of everyone.

Still, something about the guy didn't feel right. Why would he show up out of blue without calling first? And had he heard correctly that Kellie's parents had directed Karl here? Why hadn't they called?

Ryan choked down a piece of homemade bread with

butter. One way or another, he'd keep an eye on Karl. Whether Kellie liked it or not, he wasn't going to stand by and let her get hurt.

Chapter Nine

"Kellie, you know I don't allow men in your room." The frown on her landlady's face couldn't be deeper.

"I know, Mrs. Wheeler, but this is my brother from out of state. He'll only be here one night."

Mrs. Wheeler's gaze narrowed.

The resemblance was there if she'd only look. They had the same face, although Karl's looked more worn. Kellie waited, hoping her brother kept his mouth shut while he stood antsy behind her.

"One night. That's it." Mrs. Wheeler held out her hand toward her brother. "What did you say your name was?"

He stepped forward wearing his charming, fake smile. The one that made promises he'd never keep. "Karl Cavanaugh, ma'am. And thank you for letting me stay."

"Well, I'm a widow alone. You understand."

Kellie wanted to roll her eyes. Mrs. Wheeler, though old, was no weakling. Still, Kellie would protect her as best she could.

Karl's smile broadened. "Of course. And like Kellie said, only one night. I'll find a place of my own tomorrow."

Kellie glanced at him quickly. Was he planning to stay in the area? How was that going to work with Dorrie and the girls? Too many questions and not enough answers. Like why didn't her parents give her or Dorrie a heads-up? Why did they always do what Karl asked of them?

With a tired sigh, Kellie led the way. "Come on, I'll show you my room."

Karl swung his backpack over his shoulder and followed after giving Mrs. Wheeler a friendly nod.

As they made their way up the back stairs, Karl whistled. "This lady's loaded. How'd you fall into such a sweet setup?"

Kellie ignored the sudden icky feeling that she was somehow taking advantage by living here. "From the church I used to attend. Mrs. Wheeler is pretty independent, but she likes having someone here at night. I rent a room, and that's way less than an apartment."

"Convenient," Karl muttered.

True, for both of them. So, why'd he have to make her feel slimy about it? Kellie unlocked her door and opened it wide to the decent-sized room she called home. "Make yourself comfortable. You can have the bed or the futon, take your pick."

"Futon's fine."

Kellie headed for the small fridge. "Hungry?"

"Sure, whatever." Karl slipped out of his jacket and plopped onto the futon with a soft groan. Reaching for the remote to her tiny TV, he clicked it on and thumbed through channels. "Nice, you've got cable."

A nice extra from Mrs. Wheeler. Not that Kellie watched much TV. She'd been busy making something of herself. She glanced at her brother with her mind in a whirl but held her tongue as she made a couple of turkey sandwiches. She handed a plate to Karl along with a can of diet pop. When he frowned, she bristled. "Would you rather have water?"

"No. This is fine. What happened to your hand?"

"I cut it. Not a big deal." Although it throbbed a little. So did her heart at the memory of Ryan's kiss. He'd made her feel cherished and worth something. She cleared those cloying thoughts out of her mind and sat on the floor, crossing her legs under the coffee table. "Why are you here?"

Karl shrugged. "I want to see my kids."

"They have names. Hannah and Gracie. And Dorrie might not allow it."

He looked annoyed. "I know."

Kellie tipped her head. "Then why didn't you call her? Or me?"

Karl reached inside his pocket and pulled out a coin. A symbol of program completion used in a lot of treatment centers. He spun it on the tabletop and they both watched it wobble and then settle next to her paper plate.

"What's that?" Kellie played dumb. She wanted Karl to tell her that he'd graduated from rehab. For all she knew he could have stolen it.

"You know what it is. Mom and Dad told me you're interning at a treatment center."

"An outpatient center," she corrected. At least their parents had paid attention to what she'd told them she was doing.

"Whatever."

"Did you finish?"

He grabbed his sandwich. "I spent four months there."

"Are you clean?" Kellie couldn't tell if he was using. He didn't look like he was under any influence other than maybe lack of a good night's sleep.

"Yeah." Karl took a bite of the sandwich and then leaned back as if too tired to chew. He looked her square in the eyes. "I really messed up my life, Kel."

That was an understatement. He'd messed up more than only his life. Dorrie's, the girls', their parents', hers. Still, she managed a smile. "You think?"

He laughed then, but it came out bitter and twisted. Not the carefree sound she'd remembered growing up. "Thanks for letting me stay here."

"Where are you going to go tomorrow?"

He shrugged. "I don't know."

"Do you have a sponsor?" Kellie asked.

He shook his head.

Kellie knew how important it was for someone who'd completed treatment to have a support system to lean on, someone to talk to when temptation kicked in. "I'll get you set up."

Karl yawned. "Thanks."

She scrambled to her feet, half her sandwich untouched. "I'll get you a blanket, too. The bathroom's right through that door. Feel free to stretch out and fall asleep if you want. I've got some reading to do and then I'm turning in early."

He nodded. "Kellie?"

She turned. "Yeah?"

"What's with you and that big guy?"

Kellie briefly closed her eyes and her heart took a tumble. The feel of Ryan's mouth on hers wasn't something she'd soon forget. Setting her paper plate by the sink, she looked at her arms. She still wore Ryan's shirt and it hung on her, even though she'd rolled up the sleeves. "Ryan's a friend."

"Yours or Dorrie's?"

Kellie didn't mistake the edge to her brother's voice when he mentioned his ex-wife. Maybe it would be best to leave Karl in the dark about that one. "Does it matter?"

He let out a defeated-sounding sigh. "No. I guess not."

* * *

Ryan tossed pebbles at Kellie's window. A small light shone from the darkened room with two long windows nestled over the garage. That soft glow told him she was still up.

After a few seconds, Kellie lifted the window and gestured that she'd be right down then closed it again with a soft click.

He looked up at the sky. Clouds played peekaboo with a waning moon and his breath billowed like white smoke in front of him. It was cold enough for frost, and he felt chilled all the way through wearing only a light jacket without his heavy flannel shirt. But he had to know that Kellie was okay before he called it a night. Before he took the hot shower his muscles begged for and hit the sack.

"Hey." Kellie, dressed in plaid flannel pajamas underneath a knee-length coat, walked toward him with her hair loose. "Here's your shirt."

More than anything, he wanted to take her in his arms, but he knew better. "Here's your jacket."

"Thanks."

He drank in the sight of her. That gorgeous hair finally loose and wild. The delicate freckles that dusted her nose and cheeks, the pretty eyes that looked dark in the weakening moonlight. Her red-rimmed nose announced either an oncoming cold or tears. He didn't like the thought of either. "You okay?"

She cleared her throat, making him wonder how well she was keeping it together. "Fine."

He stepped toward her and picked up a curl that lay across her shoulder. He twirled it around his finger for a couple of seconds, marveling at how it twisted and held like a corkscrew when he let go. Her hair was soft and yet strong. A lot like her. "So, what's the deal with your brother?"

"You didn't say anything to Dorrie, did you?"

He shook his head. "How long is he here for?"

Kellie shrugged. "I don't know. He says he's completed treatment and wants to see the girls. I think he's sincere."

Ryan looked at the quiet house where Kellie lived. "Is he staying with you then?"

"Just for tonight. Mrs. Wheeler wasn't too happy about it either. Tomorrow, Karl will have to figure out someplace else."

Ryan took in her worried expression. And then what? Would he bother Dorrie? Despite the fancy car the guy drove, Ryan doubted Karl had any money. He'd have already booked a motel room if he had. Ryan didn't want this guy bumming money off Kellie, either—money she couldn't afford to part with. He knew she'd give it to him, and he couldn't allow that to happen. Not when he didn't trust Karl's intentions.

"Maybe he can stay with me. Until he finds something."

Kellie's eyes grew wide. "What? You don't have to do that. Karl's my concern."

He smiled and picked up that curl again. "What concerns you, concerns me, too."

She shook her head, causing the curl to pull away from his grasp. "I don't know…"

"Let me do this." He wanted to keep an eye on the guy. If Karl was serious about recovery, maybe he could help him somehow. But if Karl wasn't serious, Ryan wanted to know that, too. Besides, his house was empty.

Kellie's smile teased. "This might be another conflict of interest, you know."

"Oh, I think we smashed the ethics code pretty good tonight."

"You're not kidding." Then her eyes grew wide and worried. "Look, Ryan—"

He laid a finger against her lips. "Don't. I know it wasn't the wisest thing to do, but I'm not sorry, Kel. After I get through with group, let's explore what's going on between us. I'll wait as long as I have to."

Her expression softened, but the tempest in her gaze hadn't lessened.

He ran his thumb along the fullness of her lower lip. "I don't want to discuss all the reasons why we shouldn't. Can't we think about why we should? Eventually?"

"I don't know, maybe." She stepped back, out of reach and in control. "I'll let Karl know about your housing offer."

Ryan gave her his business card that had both his cell phone and work number on it. "If you need me, call."

"I will."

He hesitated to leave. Right now, Kellie had enough to deal with. She didn't need him pushing barriers or breaking down what had happened between them. It wasn't exactly a simple kiss. Not for him, it wasn't. "Good night, Kellie."

She looked relieved. "Good night, Ryan."

Glad he'd made the right call by leaving, Ryan walked down her landlady's driveway toward the road where he'd parked his truck. More tired than usual, he brought his shirt to his nose and inhaled. The fabric smelled like her—soft and feminine. A wisp of scent that remained out of reach; that was pure Kellie. He wanted to catch her and keep her safe.

The following afternoon, Ryan whistled softly while he took his seat at group.

Jess, the young woman with tattoos, gave him a big

grin. "Wow. Someone's in a good mood. What happened to you?"

Ryan laughed when he realized what song he'd been whistling. The same tune had been playing in the lobby of LightHouse Center when he walked in and the title sure fit.

He wiggled his eyebrows. "I kissed a girl and I liked it."

Jess's pierced eyebrows arched in surprise. "Whoa, really? Well good for you."

Reality hit. Was it good for him? He couldn't even ask Kellie out. And tonight her brother was coming to stay with him. More complications. "We'll see."

Jess narrowed her gaze and then cocked her head to the side. "You're really into this chick, aren't you?"

Ryan could easily picture Kellie bristling like a porcupine at being called a *chick*. He suspected a lot of her feistiness covered vulnerability and fear. Was her reluctance with him really about her internship or was she afraid to let herself have feelings for him, because of her past? Seeing what addiction had done to her brother must be part of her hesitation. And he'd admitted his struggle with alcohol when they'd canoed. That couldn't have helped his case.

He sighed. "Yeah, I am."

Jess gave him a wistful smile. "She's a fortunate girl."

"I hope so." Ryan knew where they were headed, but before pressing Kellie for more, he needed to be whole.

He was getting there. Group meetings made sense. Fighting the temptation to fixate on his guilt and numb the painful memories of the accident was something he still battled. A battle he'd tried to surrender to God.

Bottom line, his drinking days were done, now that he understood where it would take him if he continued. He didn't want to go there. He didn't want to become that guy.

And Kellie deserved more than jagged pieces of his heart glued back together. Could he let go of Sara's memory?

He had to if he wanted to make any kind of solid future with Kellie.

Whoa! He'd jumped way ahead of himself. Kellie wasn't exactly an open book when it came to how she felt about him. Reliving that kiss in his mind, Ryan had an idea, but would she let go of all her reservations and give them a chance?

Ryan settled in his seat with another sigh. When he looked up, he stared directly into the face of John, his group leader and Kellie's boss.

"Ryan." John gave him a nod.

With a sinking feeling in the pit of his stomach, Ryan knew he'd heard everything. Would John put two and two together? Probably. Had he just blown it for Kellie's internship? He hoped not.

They made the rounds in group, getting caught up from last week. Each person shared as needed. Ryan kept quiet, but his mind churned.

"Ryan, anything you'd like to add?" John's voice sliced through his brain.

"Not today, no. I'm holding my own out there." Ryan couldn't relax. Couldn't really focus either. He kept thinking about Kellie and what he might have accidentally done.

By the time group had finished, Ryan hung back and waited. He wanted to clarify a few things with John Thompson one-on-one. With a deep breath he approached the group leader. "You got a minute?"

John didn't look surprised by his request. "Sure. Let's go to my office."

Ryan followed and then slipped into a cushioned chair in front of John's desk.

"What's on your mind?"

Ryan got straight to the point. "You probably heard what I told Jess."

"I did." John waited.

Ryan wiped his hands on his thighs. "And you probably know who I was talking about."

"That's up to you to tell me, but be careful there." John peeked over the rims of his glasses. "I really don't want to hear a name."

Ryan got the point. John wasn't going to come down on Kellie if he didn't have to. And that was good. A huge relief even, but Ryan couldn't leave. Not yet. "I care about her, John. Seriously care."

John narrowed his gaze. "You're vulnerable right now. You could be transferring feelings you're trying to deal with, trying to get closure from."

Ryan nodded. He'd thought about that, but kissing Kellie was different. She wasn't like Sara. "I know I have to back off and finish group. Finish my master plan here. But you need to know that nothing inappropriate took place. I kissed her and that was it."

"Less than that crosses the ethical line." John's frown was deep.

Ethics. Ryan snorted. That list of professional dos and don'ts stood in the way of something beautiful that was happening between him and Kellie. Something strong and lasting. Something that might have the power to heal them both.

Ryan needed to be patient, but he also needed to be honest with the man who'd stamp his master plan complete. Giving John a grin, Ryan figured he might as well spill everything. "Well, you're really going to love this one. I've offered for her brother to stay with me. He's in recovery. Or claims to be."

John muttered. "You're really walking the tightrope here."

"I know. Got any advice on dealing with this guy?"

"Lay some ground rules, be honest and be careful. And don't be afraid to call me if you get in a jam."

Ryan stood and offered John his hand. "Thanks. I appreciate you hearing me out."

John took it with a firm shake. "Remember, you're working through your own recovery. More from grief, than a substance, but you could easily fall into relying on that substance to cope. Don't blow it."

"Got it." Ryan nodded.

He had no intention of blowing this opportunity to keep Kellie safe. And while Ryan was at it, he'd keep her safe from himself, too. Romance had to wait. For now.

Kellie took a deep breath and dialed Ryan's phone number. He'd have her cell number now. A necessity if something happened with Karl. Tossing pebbles at her window wouldn't cut it in an emergency.

"This is Ryan." His deep voice sounded warm and caring, like a man she could depend on. Trust even.

Clearing her throat, she responded. "Ryan, this is Kellie."

"Hey." That silken voice of his dipped lower, sounding softer. His lips probably curled into that sweet smile of his, too.

Think.

"When would you like me to bring Karl over? I mean, if you're still serious about housing him." Could she sound more lame? Karl was her brother, not some stray dog.

He chuckled. "Yes, I'm serious. Why don't you guys come for dinner and we can go over stuff."

Panic ripped through her. "Stuff?"

"House rules, timeline, that sort of thing."

Karl. This was about Karl. "Oh, okay. What about work at Dorrie's?"

"I called Jeff this morning to let him know I couldn't be there tonight, so he's going. He needs to take an inventory of what's left to do and what's needed to get it done."

"Great, thanks for that." Ryan was not only dependable but thoughtful, too. Because of Karl, Dorrie didn't expect her tonight either. Because of Ryan's call to Jeff, the builder who oversaw the project, work would still get done. They were covered.

"How's your hand? Did you get it checked out?"

"Not yet. But it's fine. It's healing nicely." She gathered her thoughts back to what she'd agreed to. Ryan's place for dinner. Together. With her brother. "What time and what can I bring?"

"Give me half an hour. I'm almost home. And not a thing. I've got this."

Kellie closed her eyes. She really hoped *this* didn't blow up in her face. "We'll be there. Thanks."

"No problem. And Kel?"

Her heart did a little flip. "Yeah?"

"Did you tell Dorrie?"

"She didn't take the news well, but Dorrie's willing to let Karl see the girls only if he doesn't tell them who he is."

Ryan blew out his breath with a slow whoosh. "How's that going to work?"

"We're going to make him volunteer on the house."

Ryan chuckled. "Good call."

Kellie wasn't sure she agreed with Dorrie on this one, but she'd abide by her sister-in-law's wishes. Karl had walked out on his family when Hannah was only a year old. He'd come back a couple of times but never stayed long, and Gracie was the result of Dorrie's last attempt to make something work. The girls had never known their dad, and Dorrie wanted to keep it that way.

"I guess so. See you in a few." After Kellie ended the call with Ryan, she glanced at her watch. Where was Karl?

This morning, she'd left him asleep on the futon in order to grab more than cereal for breakfast. She'd called out from Beth's school with a personal matter excuse because she really couldn't leave her brother on his own all day at Mrs. Wheeler's.

This afternoon, Karl had gone into town to look around. Kellie made use of her brother's absence and called Ginny for a list of possible sponsors she could give him. She'd prepare for her brother sticking around even though he had a pattern of bolting. He didn't let anyone get close, either.

Fingering the treatment program completion coin Karl had left on her coffee table, Kellie prayed her brother would see his recovery through. He seemed different this time. Maybe he'd finally hit rock bottom and was ready to get serious about changing his life.

At the sound of a car pulling in, Kellie looked out the window to the driveway below. Karl was back in the nick of time. She raced down to meet him and tell him about their dinner plans. But by the time they pulled into Ryan's driveway and parked, Kellie hoped they weren't late. It was cold, and Kellie pulled the collar of her coat close when she got out of the car.

"Nice place," Karl said.

"Yeah." Kellie glanced at the single story cottage with a huge back deck and a perfect view of the lake. The property was neat and tidy and obviously well cared for.

Ryan's canoe had been put up under the rafters of a roof overhang from a huge storage shed. Stacks of firewood were nestled between the poles. A large fire pit had been constructed halfway to the water's edge. A lonely rustic chair sat empty but looked well-worn. How often did Ryan sit out here watching the dying embers of a fire, alone?

"You coming?" Karl had gone to the door while she gawked.

Kellie caught up and knocked on the door.

"Come in." Ryan opened it wide. The fragrant smell of roasted meat and warmth from a crackling fire in a huge stone hearth drew them inside. "I hope you like pot roast."

"When did you make that?" Kellie's jaw dropped.

"Crock-Pot." He gave her a wink and then took their coats. "Make yourselves at home. I've got a couple of things to do yet."

"Need help?" Kellie asked.

"Nope. Karl, you can put your stuff in the red bedroom."

"Thanks, man. I appreciate this."

"No problem." Ryan words might be light, but his eyes looked grave. This was serious, and he did it for her.

Kellie gave Ryan a grateful nod and then followed her brother with his backpack and one duffel bag and gawked even more.

Ryan's home wasn't big, but he'd made the most of the space. He'd kept things simple and clean with hardwood floors and wooly area rugs. The overstuffed plaid furniture gave it a casual feel, but the richly colored walls of red and coffee were a surprise for a bachelor's home.

Curious, she peeked into the other bedroom. *His.* There was a big bed sporting a navy quilt, a bedside table with a lamp and a clock and that was about it. No picture frames anywhere. No artwork. The only thing hanging on the wall was a flat-screen TV. Where were pictures of his dead fiancée?

The other rooms were pretty bare when it came to knickknacks as well. Maybe he wasn't finished with his upgrades. The work looked freshly completed.

Kellie wound her way back to the open kitchen, living and dining room combination. "You did all this?"

Ryan shrugged as he placed the steaming Crock-Pot on the table. "Yeah. Everything was pretty ancient when I bought this place, but the structure was solid. I think we're ready to eat."

Over dinner, Ryan laid out his house rules for Karl. Pretty simple really—no drugs, no alcohol and no lies. It wasn't the most comfortable meal, but she held her tongue while the guys hashed out a rooming plan.

Listening to them was like watching a couple of game-cocks circle each other, looking for weaknesses. By the time dinner was over, Kellie wasn't sure if this would work, but Karl had few options and Ryan was adamant to give it a try. Besides, it was only temporary—until Karl found a job and someplace else to live.

Kellie dried her hands on a dish towel. She'd cleaned up while Ryan showed Karl the ropes with the multimedia options on the TV and then the damper on the fireplace.

Maybe she should let the two men get used to each other. "Well, I guess I'll call it a night. Thanks for everything, Ryan."

"You're welcome to hang out."

She shook her head but stepped close to the warmth of a real wood-burning hearth. Tempting thought. Before turning to grab her coat, Kellie noticed a couple of picture frames tucked away on shelves built into the walls on either side of the stone chimney.

One of the photos was an old family portrait. She quickly recognized Ryan's parents and brother and a young girl who must be Ryan's sister. Her stomach tightened at the sight of the next picture.

It was a fairly recent one of Ryan with a giant smile holding up a young woman's hand that sported a good-sized diamond on her ring finger. Kellie stared into the laughing dark eyes of Ryan's fiancée. She resembled her sister, Hope, but her features were not quite as fine nor did she wear any makeup. Sara looked full of life. Warm and pretty in a natural, outdoorsy sort of way.

"That's Sara." Ryan stood close behind her.

"Yeah." They both looked so happy and deeply in love. Kellie's throat felt dry and tight. "Surely this isn't the only picture you have of her?"

"It's the only one I have out."

Kellie turned to face him. "Why?"

He shrugged. "Too hard to look at them."

It was still hard. She could see it in his eyes. He wasn't over her at all.

"I'll walk you out."

Kellie nodded. Grabbing her coat, she said good-night to her brother and then followed Ryan outside to the deck. She'd walk home; it wasn't far. Tiny snowflakes fell but disappeared when they hit the ground, crinkling the dry leaves that lay everywhere.

"November came in with a vengeance. Man, it's cold." Ryan shoved his hands in his jean pockets.

"Why didn't you wear a coat?"

He didn't answer but stepped toward her. "I need to tell you something."

Kellie held her breath, while her heart skipped erratically. "Okay."

"I told your boss about all this."

Kellie felt her fists clench. "All this?"

"Your brother staying with me, and, uh, that kiss."

"What?" She opened her hands before she pounded him.

"I had to." Ryan looked her in the eyes without remorse.

Kellie knew honesty was a huge part of group dynamics and recovery. Expecting Ryan to hide their burgeoning relationship was wrong of her. Getting involved with him was wrong, too. With all her training, she should know better. And now Karl living with him was stepping way over the line.

"I'm taking advantage of you," she whispered.

"How?" Ryan's brow furrowed. "I wouldn't have offered a place for your brother if I didn't want to do it. I wouldn't have kissed you without wanting to, either."

She'd wanted to kiss Ryan, too. In fact, she still wanted to. "It doesn't make it right."

"Says who?"

"Says everything I've read about it." Thinking of all her classes, and the manual code of ethics that every counselor proudly displayed in their offices, Kellie wondered if she knew anything at all. What she felt for Ryan was real. It had nothing to do with power or control. If anything, she felt completely out of control.

"It's okay, Kel. It'll be okay."

Kellie shook her head. She wasn't so sure. But then, she'd find out when she showed up for work at Light-House Center.

Chapter Ten

By Thursday afternoon at LightHouse Center, Kellie was stumped. Her boss had not once brought up what Ryan had told him. Was he protecting a client's privacy or letting the whole thing go? Surely she deserved to be reprimanded for getting personally involved with a client while she was an intern.

Her internship was more or less finished, but was she home free? She closed her eyes, calling herself every kind of coward for not going into John's office to find out. The need to know what her boss was going to do gnawed at her, but that didn't make her feet move.

Kellie chewed the short nail of her pinky finger and stared at the phone. Rallying the courage to call John's extension, she jumped when her cell phone rang instead. Recognizing the caller as the school in Traverse City, Kellie answered before the second ring.

Bracing for bad news, Kellie blinked twice when she heard the opposite. They wanted to hire her as long as she passed her certification test. Those scores were due to be posted online the following day. She couldn't access the printable files for a few more days, but at least she'd know if she passed. And if she did, the job was hers.

All hers.

After she ended the call, tears gathered in her eyes, blurring her vision. "Thank You, Lord," she whispered, and then hung her head in her hands.

She heard soft footsteps on the carpeted floor behind her and then felt a hand touch her shoulder. Ginny.

"Oh no, Kellie, what is it?" Ginny slipped onto the corner of her desk.

Kellie looked up with a grin and croaked, "I got the job."

Ginny gripped the collar of her sweater. "You gave me a scare. I thought...oh, never mind."

Kellie grabbed a tissue, blew her nose and then sniffed. "What did you think?"

Ginny rolled her eyes. "I thought it was, you know, romance trouble."

Kellie's eyes grew wide and she sputtered, "But I'm not, that is..."

Ginny only raised an eyebrow, but her eyes held warmth not censure.

Kellie felt her cheeks turning red. Surely Ryan hadn't talked to Ginny, too, but maybe John had. Who all knew about her and Ryan anyway?

Ginny smiled. "You have to tell John."

"I will. Right now." Kellie stood and squared her shoulders. Was this why he hadn't made a fuss over Ryan? Did John already know the job was hers?

Leaving Ginny behind, Kellie rushed down the hall. John's door was halfway ajar and she could see him staring out the window while drinking a huge cup of his awful coffee.

She tapped her knuckles against the wood. "Got a minute?"

John swung his chair around and smiled. "I do. Come in."

Kellie clenched and unclenched her fingers. "Well, I got the job."

John smiled again but didn't look surprised. "Good for you. When do you start?"

"After Thanksgiving. As long as I passed my test and successfully complete my internship." She looked at him and waited.

Nothing but silent consideration from the man in the chair.

"Will I successfully complete my internship?" Her voice wobbled.

John chuckled. "I don't see why not."

"Even after what Ryan told you?" Kellie blurted.

"Ah, yes. Ryan." John set down his mug of coffee.

A shiver of alarm traveled up Kellie's spine as she slipped into a chair. John's office was large but unassuming. Two windows on connecting corner walls gave a nice view of the small river that flowed from Lake Leelanau. She could see the dark silhouettes of tree branches stretching toward a cold November sun.

She tucked both her hands under her thighs to keep them still and waited. One of the many things she'd learned at LightHouse Center was that John was not a man to be rushed.

Finally, John let out a sigh. "Ryan's doing well. He's processing his grief."

"Yes." Kellie knew that but braced for the reprimand that was bound to come. Should come.

"Can I speak off-the-record and not as your supervisor?"

Kellie swallowed hard. "Absolutely."

"My suggestion is to keep your distance until he's done here. Until you can be sure his feelings for you are stable."

Kellie felt like her chest had been put into a vise that

kept cranking tighter and tighter. What did that mean? Ryan wasn't over Sara. That had to be it. "I've come to that same conclusion."

John leaned forward. "Don't misunderstand me. Ryan's a good man, Kellie. But I would hate to see either of you get hurt because you pushed things too soon."

Kellie cocked her head. "He said he'd wait."

"Some people are worth waiting for, and if not, you'll know because you kept a clear head." John wasn't warning her away from Ryan at all. And that spoke volumes. But she could sense that he wasn't telling her everything. There was more to his concerns then he was showing.

"You don't think he's over his fiancée?" Kellie narrowed her gaze.

He didn't blink an eye, and she knew John wasn't at liberty to share that with her. Not now, after she'd crossed the line into a personal relationship with Ryan. Not when she wasn't part of their therapy group. But John had effectively warned her to protect her heart for now. Why?

Who was she trying to kid? Her heart was already engaged, but not completely given. She stood to leave, feeling more unsettled than when she first came in. "I get it. Wait this thing out."

John nodded.

At his office door, Kellie turned and smiled. She'd received some fatherly advice she hadn't expected from a boss. Good advice, too. Being certain never caused anyone harm. That's all John was saying. Rushing ahead was for fools. Kellie liked to think she was no fool. "Thank you, John."

"My pleasure." He gave her an encouraging smile.

Kellie wanted to ask if she should fear alcohol dependence but knew that answer as well. She'd interned long enough to learn that once a person abused a substance to numb their pain, there was always the possibility they'd do so again in the future. Part of working recovery was about facing what lay underneath that need to self-medicate. To numb.

Ryan was working on that through group, but he wasn't home free. Not yet. Maybe that's what John was trying to tell her without telling her. And that meant she wasn't home free either.

"Hold it still." Ryan drilled the screw halfway in place and then stopped. Hanging cupboards was tricky business. He wanted them straight, and Karl wasn't exactly laser beam focused on the task. The guy must have either ADHD or ants in his pants.

"Hope," Ryan called out when he spotted her walking through the kitchen with a steaming covered dish. Dinner would be served in the living room tonight because the kitchen was torn up. "Does this look straight?"

She narrowed her gaze and then shook her head. "Up a titch on your left."

"A titch?" Karl gave him an amused look.

Ryan grimaced as he shifted the block of heavy cabinetry. "How's that?"

"Perfect." Hope nodded and then disappeared.

"Hold it still," Ryan had to remind Karl. The guy's attention followed the food, and he couldn't really blame him. Something smelled incredible.

Karl had been working with him on the house for a week now. Every day Ryan had left early from the research center because November was slow and his duties were light. He and Karl had come to the construction site every afternoon. Sinclair often joined them.

Ryan was grateful for his brother's help and influence. He had to hand it to Sinclair for interspersing spiritual lessons while they worked. Karl seemed to soak it in, but then he'd get this blank look on his face like nothing had stuck. Did he think God's saving grace didn't apply to him?

Drilling in the rest of the screws, Ryan stepped off the platform and took a good hard look. Hope had been correct and the cabinets finally looked straight.

"Ryan and Karl, the cake is here." Gracie twirled her way into the kitchen wearing a sparkly purple skirt over pink sweatpants.

"Shh." Ryan placed his finger to his lips in a gesture he hoped would make the kid quiet down. "It's supposed to be a surprise."

Gracie slapped her hand over her mouth and giggled.

"Blabbermouth," Ryan muttered.

"Am not." Gracie put her hands on her hips and jutted out her chin.

"She looks just like her mother when she does that." Karl's voice sounded strangled and full of regret.

Ryan looked more closely at the seven-year-old. Both girls favored their mom, with dark blond hair and brown eyes. There wasn't much of a resemblance to Karl that he could see. Considering Dorrie's request to hide Karl's identity, that was a good thing.

And so far, Karl had abided by Dorrie's request. The girls had no idea who he was other than another guy volunteering to help. Ryan felt bad about that. Seemed like the girls should know their father, but then Dorrie had her reasons. And from what Kellie had told him, Karl had never been around. But Ryan suspected that Hannah might already know. He'd caught her studying Karl one too many times.

Ryan tousled Gracie's hair. "Where's your aunt Kellie?"

"Painting my bedroom." Gracie grinned, the insult completely forgotten.

Ryan stepped out of the way of a huge sheet cake with the words *Congratulations Kellie* written in blue icing being carried inside by Dorrie and his aunt Jamee.

"Where to?" his aunt asked.

"Follow me." Ryan cleared space on one of the card tables. "Thanks for doing this on such short notice."

"Baking a banana cake for my nephew's girl is my pleasure." She craned her neck and looked around. "Where is the beauty?"

"She's coming. Hope's gathering everyone." Ryan didn't bother to correct his aunt that Kellie wasn't his girl.

But then he'd been the only one Kellie told about her job offer. She'd asked him not to say anything until it was a sure thing, after she'd not only seen her passing test scores but had forwarded them in writing to the school. That had happened yesterday.

He watched as Kellie walked into the living room, and her eyes lit up with surprise when she saw the huge layered cake. She glanced at Dorrie, who pointed his way.

Kellie looked at him with softened eyes and mouthed the words *thank you*.

He didn't look away. He couldn't. Yeah, he was definitely falling hard. They'd been tiptoeing around each other all week. Pretending there was nothing between them but friendship.

"Kel, I'd like you to meet my aunt Jamee."

"It's a pleasure. You take care of this boy. He's a keeper." His aunt pulled Kellie into her arms for a hug.

Kellie's panicked eyes widened and never left his face.

Ryan laughed. Didn't Kellie realize she'd already passed the test with his mom? Kellie was a slam dunk with the rest of the Marsh family.

"Well, Kellie, are you going to tell us your big news?" one of the volunteers asked.

"I got the job I'd interviewed for at a school in Traverse City. I start in a couple of weeks."

The group cheered, and Ryan's aunt got busy cutting and serving cake after Sinclair said a blessing over the food. The celebratory mood grew more noisy and excited with each piece of cake consumed. The house was on schedule for completion, and the builder in charge promised to bring in his crew for any last-minute finishing. They'd make sure Dorrie and her girls had a place to move into before Christmas.

Ryan glanced at Karl. The guy looked at his daughters like he was trying to memorize their faces. Wasn't he planning on sticking around? A swell of fury gripped him. Surely Karl wasn't going to walk away from his family again.

He felt a touch to his arm. It was Kellie.

"What's got you looking like a thundercloud?"

He shook his head. "Thoughts."

"Anything you want to share?"

He steered her away from everyone so they could sit on a couple of folding chairs near the far wall. Still, he kept his voice low. "I don't get your brother."

Alarm shone from her eyes. "Anything more specific?"

"He had everything and blew it."

Kellie nodded and moved her food around the plate with her fork. "It's been that way for a long time. But I think he's finally trying to change."

Ryan wasn't so sure. He had nothing to go by other than a gut feeling. "How can you tell?"

"He's working on this house for one thing."

Ryan didn't point out that it was because they'd forced Karl into it in exchange for seeing his daughters. Ryan had also reinforced that Karl's free lodging depended on how well he did here. He didn't appreciate the guy's indifference or halfway approach to getting things done right. Didn't he care that his daughters would live here?

"And he's meeting with a sponsor," Kellie said around a mouthful of lasagna. She didn't eat her cake first. A small slice lay perched on the side of her paper plate.

She wanted her brother to succeed. He did, too. Only Ryan wasn't sure that Karl wanted it. What Karl did in the mornings while he was at work, Ryan could only guess. He was supposed to be looking for work; the guy was on the phone enough. But then Karl went out some evenings to meet friends. For a guy who hadn't grown up around here, Karl had made *friends* awfully fast.

Ryan had never smelled alcohol when Karl returned, only the lingering stench of cigarette smoke. But then if he were taking drugs, they might not have a smell. Ryan didn't know. Karl never stayed out late, so maybe it was okay. Maybe he *was* working his recovery, even if he was private about it. As Kellie said, Karl had a sponsor he met with.

"That's good then." Ryan shouldn't make a mountain out of a molehill.

Kellie nodded. "How's group?"

He grinned at her. "Do you miss interning?"

She shrugged. "A little, maybe. And you totally side-stepped my question."

He hadn't meant to. She seemed eager to know, or maybe it was more about how close he was to finishing. And that gave him hope. "I think I'm doing well, but John thinks I'm rushing through it."

"Are you?"

"I want to move on." He wanted to move on with her.

She gave him a hard look, one that made him uncomfortable.

"I'm serious, Kel. I'm not blowing this off. Even if I

don't talk a lot in group, I listen and try to apply what I hear. When I put my mind to something, I get it done."

She looked pleased. Sweeping her arm to encompass their surroundings, she smiled. "I can see that."

He focused on her mouth, wishing they were anywhere but in a room full of people. He cupped her cheek and gently ran his thumb over her full bottom lip. "I know what I feel, too."

She leaned a little into the palm of his hand. "Yeah?"

"Yeah." Ryan might not openly share his feelings, but he didn't question them. "I think I'm falling for you."

He'd known Sara was the one for him by the time he was sixteen years old. He'd never wavered from that truth. He'd been sure then, and he was sure now.

Kellie blinked. Had she heard him correctly? Warmth pooled into the pit of her belly. But he couldn't be in love with her after only a few weeks. It was too fast. The advice given by her boss nearly a week ago rang in her ears. Pretty hard to follow it when looking into Ryan's dark eyes.

She wanted to confess the same thing, but something held her back. "I care about you, too."

Ryan dropped his hand. Obviously that hadn't been the answer he'd wanted to hear. "Well, it's a start, I suppose."

Kellie tried for clarity of thought. John had said it was too soon to trust Ryan's feelings as stable. "You're the one who promised to wait."

He smiled. "True."

She heard the murmur of voices from outside and looked around. "Where's Karl?"

"I don't know. Smoke break?" Ryan peered out the window and then gestured toward the backyard.

She noticed that Dorrie wasn't around either. When

she heard the angry sound of raised voices, her stomach sank. "I'll be back."

Ryan heard them, too, and stood. "I'll go with you."

"No. I've got this." Kellie grabbed her coat and flew out the back door.

"You agreed!" Dorrie's voice sliced through the cold night air.

Karl took a menacing step toward his ex-wife. "What did you expect me to do? I wanted to see my kids."

Kellie stepped between them. "Whoa. There's a houseful in there and they can probably hear you, so let's keep it down. What's going on?"

"My kids have a right to know who I am," Karl snarled.

"I knew this was a mistake." Muttering, Dorrie paced the backyard and then glared at Karl. "You ruin everything you touch. Leave them alone."

"They're my girls."

"No, they're mine," Dorrie asserted. "You've never been a father to them. I've struggled to keep a roof over their heads no thanks to you."

"I did what I could." Was her brother spoiling for a fight? What was wrong with him? Dorrie had him beat on all fronts.

"Why'd you come here, Karl? Why now?" Dorrie's voice dropped low.

Kellie watched her brother's face change from anger to sorrowful regret before becoming a blank page. He nodded and cursed. "I'm outta here."

She glanced at Dorrie.

"Let him go. And I don't want to see him back here, either." Her sister-in-law headed for the house.

Kellie rushed down the driveway toward her brother. It didn't take long to catch up. She reached out and grabbed his arm. "Wait."

He whipped away from her. "What do you want?"

"What are you trying to do?"

"They're my kids, Kel. She has no right."

Kellie gasped and then sputtered. "Are you serious? She has every right. Dorrie raised those girls on her own with no child support from you. She could have filed, but didn't. Why's that?"

Her brother shrugged. "I sent her money when I could."

Kellie knew how infrequent that had been. "Do you realize how showing up with that expensive car is a slap in the face for her? She's struggled, Karl. Dorrie works hard and she's protective. I can't say I blame her. If you're serious about being a dad in their lives, why can't you wait it out until you prove that you're sticking around?"

Her brother shrugged. "I don't have that kind of time."

Alarm skittered through her. "What are you saying? Are you sick or something?"

His gaze slipped away from hers. "I've always been sick. Just forget it." He started for his car.

Kellie followed, but fear for him crawled through her insides and chilled her to the bone. "Talk to me, Karl."

But her brother waved her off like she meant absolutely nothing to him and kept walking.

Tears stung her eyes. She'd worshipped the ground Karl walked on when they were kids. She'd followed him like a puppy dog and he'd never chased her way because he'd watched over her while their parents were at the office or showing houses.

Oh, sometimes he told her to get lost when his friends came over, but if Karl went somewhere, he'd take her along. Sledding, bike rides, she'd been a part of everything he did while their parents were away. He'd been the one to take off her training wheels while Mom and Dad were busy making money.

"There comes a time when you have to stop being scared, Kel," he'd told her before unscrewing the bolts on those wheels.

She remembered listening to him, finding strength from the confidence he'd had in her. Why had everything gone wrong when Karl turned thirteen? He'd stopped loving her and she'd been so scared that she'd done something wrong. That she'd pushed him away somehow.

"You okay?" Ryan stood behind her.

She sniffed. "Some counselor I'll make. I can't even get my own brother to talk to me."

Ryan turned her around and pulled her into his arms. "You're an awesome counselor, Kellie. But you know you can't make anyone talk if they don't want to or if they're not ready. Let him go cool off and then try again."

She nodded. Her nose fit into the neckline of Ryan's flannel shirt, and she breathed deep the woodsy, cedar-like scent of him.

He kissed the top of her head.

She pulled back. "Thanks."

"It's okay to need a shoulder to cry on, Kellie. It's okay to need."

"Not for me, it isn't."

He shook his head, but he didn't understand how much it hurt to have her needs ignored like they didn't matter. Like she didn't matter. Ryan came from a supportive family with parents who'd always been there for him. Who'd never let him down.

Kellie caressed Ryan's cheek. "You're a good man."

He turned his head and kissed her palm. "Kel—"

"I'm scared, Ryan. Give me time to trust you, okay?"

He gave her the sweetest look of understanding. "Okay. Take all the time you need. I'm not going anywhere."

But only time would tell if that was true.

* * *

By the time Ryan was ready to lock up Dorrie's house and call it a night, there was only him and his brother left. They looked around at the progress they'd made in such a short time.

Sinclair whistled. "This is really shaping up."

Thinking about what Karl must have put Kellie through, Ryan realized how good he had it. He put a hand on his brother's shoulder. "Thank you. Thanks for being here."

"Hey, no problem."

"I'm serious. You've done more than I ever expected. Both you and Hope, but especially you. We wouldn't be this far without your help and the guys you brought out."

"You're my brother, and Dorrie's a church member. It's the kind of thing we're supposed to do, right?"

Ryan nodded. "Look, when you came home—"

Sinclair held up a hand. "You don't have to say anything. I understand."

"No, I do have to say it." Ryan had to get this out. It was part of the process, one of the twelve steps, and something he needed to be released from. "I'm sorry for the way I acted when you came home. I'm sorry I held on to my anger about you leaving."

Sinclair nodded. "I'm sorry I wasn't here when you needed me."

For years Ryan refused to forgive his brother, and he'd turned the dirt on guilt's bitter worm enough. It was never his brother's place to heal this pain. It was God's. Ryan had to give this over to God, because he was done with it. He had to let it go. Ryan pulled his brother into a bear hug. "I forgive you. Please forgive me, too."

Sinclair squeezed once, really hard, before pulling back. "I do and...I love you, man."

Ryan laughed. "Okay, now we're getting sappy, but I love you, too."

Sinclair laughed and then slapped him on the shoulder.

"I think I should talk with the Petersens." Ryan wanted closure with Sara's parents. He'd avoided them long enough.

"Come to church."

"Yeah, I will." Ryan no longer needed to stay away.

He waved good-night to his brother as he checked the builder's trailer to make sure it was locked. Dorrie's place had electricity now, and they'd filled the propane tank so they'd have heat. So far, November had been downright cold.

Ryan climbed into his truck and rubbed his cold hands together. He wasn't sure whether to hope Karl was home at his place or gone completely. Regardless, he fought back anger toward the guy who'd messed up Kellie's head.

Driving down the road, he headed toward town and the mini-mart gas station to fill up his tank. He wouldn't mind one of those hot chocolates either. The glass beer case held no power over him. He was done with that, too.

After paying, Ryan climbed back into his truck and pulled forward. A couple of running vehicles parked in the empty lot next to the mini-mart caught his eye. He narrowed his gaze. One of those cars looked like Karl's.

Ryan watched and waited, for what he didn't know.

Two men talked from their open driver's side windows. And then they exchanged something, waved and pulled out.

Was it Karl?

Ryan shifted into gear and followed the Lexus sedan. Sure enough, the car turned on to Lakeshore Drive. Ryan continued to tail Karl until the guy pulled into the driveway and home. He ignored the ill feeling that nearly over-whelmed him.

Pulling in behind Karl, Ryan parked and got out. "Hey, everything okay?"

"Yeah, why?"

Ryan's mind raced. "You left early."

Karl shrugged. "Dorrie didn't want me there."

Ryan wanted to scream at Karl that he'd blown it royally but kept quiet. At least the guy looked like he'd calmed down.

Karl grabbed a small grocery sack and headed up the steps. "I got some chips and pop if you want some."

"Yeah, sure." Ryan unlocked his door and they both went inside. Was he making something out of nothing?

Shedding his coat and boots, Ryan went in search of his slippers before starting a fire. Walking by Karl's room, he noticed the door was open and a wad of cash lay on the dresser. One of those bills, the outside one, had Ben Franklin in the middle.

Ryan's stomach dropped to the soles of his feet. Where could Karl have gotten that much cash? What exactly had he witnessed there in that parking lot—a drug deal?

Chapter Eleven

"What happened back there at the mini-mart?" Ryan couldn't let this go. No way.

Karl pulled the bag of chips out of the grocery sack. "What are you talking about?"

"I saw you parked in your car next to another car."

Karl's eyes narrowed. "Yeah, so? I met with my sponsor."

That's not what it looked like to Ryan. Didn't sponsors meet with their *clients* over coffee? Drug deals went down in parked cars and empty lots and alley ways. But this was LeNaro. This was Northern Michigan with wide-open spaces, orchards and farmland. There shouldn't be drug dealers up here. "Then what did you exchange?"

"That's none of your business."

"Hey, you're living in my house. It's my business to know if you're using."

Karl sneered. "What are you, my father now? I'm way older than you."

He didn't act like it. Ryan clenched his jaw to keep from arguing with the guy. John had said to be honest, so Ryan stared him down. "Are you using drugs, Karl?"

Kellie's brother launched a vulgar, verbal bomb into the air.

Ryan ignored the expletive and again tamped down his anger. Karl should be thankful that he didn't toss his sorry carcass out the door. For Kellie's sake, Ryan tried a more diplomatic approach. "Look, I'm trying to help you here. Kellie's trying to help—"

"Leave her out of this."

Ryan was surprised by the fury in Karl's eyes. "You know I can't do that."

"Fine. Call her. She can check up on me and find out that I met with my sponsor at that mini-mart." Karl grabbed his chips and pop, headed for his room and slammed the door.

Ryan felt the churning of uncertainty in his gut. Had he been mistaken in what he saw? Running a hand through his hair, Ryan grabbed his cell phone and dialed Kellie. She'd verify her brother's claim. They'd have to figure out what to do if it wasn't true, but either way, Ryan wouldn't sleep until he knew.

Kellie fidgeted in one of the back pews before church waiting for Ryan when her cell phone vibrated. "Hi, Mom."

"How's Karl?"

Kellie fought the urge to reply that she was fine and thanks for asking. "As good as can be expected, I suppose."

"And that guy he's living with, is he okay, I mean a good influence on your brother?"

"Ryan's good." Kellie wasn't about to tell her mother that Ryan had confronted Karl on what he *thought* he saw last night. Or that they'd agreed to meet early at church to discuss it.

"Hey." Ryan scooted into the pew next to her.

Kellie nodded. "Mom, I've got to go. Church is going to start soon."

"Okay, give my love to your brother."

Kellie rolled her eyes. "Don't you call him?"

"Yes, but you know what I mean. Love you, too, honey."

She was the afterthought and always had been. Kellie sat back against the pew.

"Everything okay with your folks?"

"Same as ever."

Kellie turned toward him. She wasn't sure whether to read him the riot act or hug him for his diligence in keeping Karl on the straight and narrow. She'd been shocked by the fierce sense of loyalty to her brother when Ryan had called her last night. She'd even argued with him. She didn't want to accept the possibility of what Ryan had seen. Is that how her parents had felt all those years? But Kellie hadn't ignored Ryan's speculation. She'd called Karl's sponsor and confirmed his story.

"So, am I a jerk?"

She tipped her head. "No, why?"

"You're looking at me like I am."

"I'm glad you're keeping a close eye on Karl, really I am, but part of me resents it, too. When can I trust his recovery?"

"When will you trust mine?" Ryan laid his hand over hers on the pew.

Her stomach flipped over. It was a good question, one she couldn't answer. Wouldn't answer now. She pulled her hand back. This was about her brother, not them. "I checked with Karl's sponsor and they did meet at the mini-mart around the time you saw him."

"So where did he get at least one hundred-dollar bill?"

Kellie's hackles rose. "I gave him three hundred dollars."

"That you don't have." Ryan's disapproval settled between them like a fence. Tall and strong.

"My first paycheck will make up for it." It'd take at least another month to see that paycheck, but she'd get by on her teacher's aide pay and credit cards. She wasn't finished working with the second-grade class until the week of Thanksgiving.

Ryan sighed. "Isn't Karl supposed to be looking for work?"

"Yeah, but we both know that takes time, and well, I want to help him as much as I can." Why did she defend him?

She felt so inadequate sometimes. If she couldn't read between the lines here, with her own brother, what good would she be to the students she hoped to serve?

She'd been through counseling. She had a bachelor's in psychology and now a master's degree as well as training and internships. Kellie knew the drill. She knew what to expect, but that didn't mean she liked it.

She'd always hated the phrase, *once an addict, always an addict but you can live sober.* Hated it because she didn't want the *always* part to be true. It meant one step away from relapse and disaster instead of being cured.

How did a person trust another to remain sober? Karl had relapsed so many times. Maybe he'd never really tried. She believed Karl was sincere this time, but was that enough?

Ryan grabbed her hand again and squeezed. "We're both trying to help him. But it's ultimately up to him to see it through."

"I know." She laced her fingers through his, but worry gnawed at her.

Maybe she should have stayed home from church this morning. She could have taken Karl out to breakfast so they could have talked. She could have made sure he was okay about Dorrie.

Kellie vaguely heard the church bell ring, announcing the start of the service. She stood along with the rest of the congregation as the worship team belted out their first of many songs that blurred in her mind.

At greeting time, Kellie shook hands with those around her while Ryan made a beeline for the Petersens. Teresa Petersen gave him a hug, and Kellie guessed that Ryan was finally going to talk to them about Sara. That he was making plans to do so. Ryan was sincere, too, but was that enough for her to believe in him and trust him with her future?

With her heart?

By the time everyone was seated for the scripture reading from 1 Corinthians 13, Kellie opened her Bible to follow along and verse 7 jumped out at her.

Love never gives up, never loses faith, is always hopeful, and endures through every circumstance.

Over and over she read that verse. The translation wasn't the same as what was being read, but Kellie knew this version was meant for her. She'd learned to expect the worst from people—her folks, her brother—and she feared she'd do the same with Ryan. She'd find a way to ruin their relationship if he didn't do it first.

She closed her eyes and breathed a crushing prayer for help. *Please Lord, show me how to believe.*

Ryan slipped back into the pew next to Kellie. He took her hand and held fast, glad she didn't let go. Glad he'd finally asked the Petersens if he could talk with them. Glad he'd been wrong about Kellie's brother.

Last night after he'd finished his phone conversation with Kellie, he'd remembered the bottle of pain meds pushed to the back of the narrow linen closet in his bathroom. Sure enough, the prescription meds he'd been given for his wisdom teeth were still there and intact.

He threw them in the trash outside and sealed up the bag ready for Monday's pickup while mentally kicking himself for not tossing them sooner. If Karl had found them, it could have been bad. But if Karl had seen them and left them alone, well, then maybe Kellie was right about Karl's seriousness in working his recovery.

Throughout Sinclair's message, Ryan kept a hold of Kellie's hand. He didn't want to let go. Ever. Silly maybe, but although he'd promised to wait, he hoped it wouldn't be long before he could pursue her. And love her openly.

When they stood to sing the hymn "Blessed Assurance" as the last song before exiting the church, Kellie glanced at him and smiled. In that moment, Ryan wanted a new future. One that stretched ahead of him for a lifetime filled with Kellie next to him singing hymns with her slightly off-key voice.

And then it hit him what Sara had meant before she'd died, and that understanding made his knees weak and his eyes burn. Had God revealed this truth, or had Ryan's ears finally opened up to hear God's voice whisper through his heart? Either way, he was grateful.

Overwhelmed by the clarity in his soul and the lump in his throat, Ryan squeezed Kellie's hand and closed his eyes. Maybe now, he could finally let Sara go. It's what she'd have wanted. She'd wanted him to be free to love again. That reality made him tremble.

Kellie leaned close. "Hey, is everything okay?"

He nodded, not sure he could speak. With service breaking up and folks filling the aisles, this wasn't the place to pull Kellie into his arms and explain. It'd keep for later.

"I saw you with the Petersens at greeting time."

Ryan wiped at his eyes and cleared his throat, but his

voice felt thick as he said, "Yeah. I'm heading over there in a little bit."

Kellie smiled up at him with what looked like pride, and as they made their way toward the back of the church, she leaned close again. "Call me if you need me. You know, like after you get back."

"Thanks. I will." He had a lot to tell her.

Ryan drove home from the Petersens' against a bracing wind that had suddenly whipped up. He was emotionally spent but felt good. He felt free. The sky loomed low and dark. It suddenly dumped tiny white crystals of sleet that ricocheted off his windshield and danced along the road until lines of it formed on the tarmac's shoulder. A good day to stay inside by the fire.

With Kellie.

Ryan almost laughed. And her brother...

He slowed down to pull into his driveway and noticed that Karl's Lexus wasn't there. Not unusual. Kellie had said they might go out to lunch. Stepping inside the quiet house, Ryan shucked off his jacket and checked the answering machine. No messages. He stacked kindling onto the grate and lit a match then smiled with satisfaction when, seconds later, yellow flames licked the dry pieces of wood.

After throwing a log onto the now-crackling fire, Ryan went into his room to change into sweats. Sleet beat against the windows, echoing through the still house. The door to Karl's room was wide open. Odd.

Ryan peeked inside.

The bed had been made, but there was no clutter on the dresser like usual. Stepping farther into the bedroom, Ryan flung open the closet door. It was empty, too. Next he checked the dresser drawers. All empty.

Dashing back into the living room, Ryan looked around.

His heart pumped with regret. Had he caused the guy to take off without so much as a note? And then he zeroed in on a single piece of paper in the kitchen near the sink. He grabbed it and read.

Ryan,
Thanks for letting me bunk here awhile, but I can't stay. Old habits are too strong and I can't be what I want to be. Take care of Kellie. All I came for was my kids. I wanted to see them one last time.
K.

Ryan crinkled the note in his hands as dread filled the pit of his stomach. Grabbing his cell phone, he dialed Dorrie.

When she didn't pick up, he got worried. Really worried.

He reread the last two lines and was nearly sick. *Please God, not that.*

He tried Karl's number and it also went straight to voice mail. Scratching his head, Ryan knew something was wrong. He dialed Kellie, knowing it was a waste of time but hoping beyond hope that her brother was there, with her.

"Hey." Her voice sounded soft.

"Is Karl with you?"

"No, why?"

"He's gone, Kellie."

He heard her sigh. "He always does this."

"Call Dorrie and make sure she's alright."

"Why?" There was real panic in her voice now.

"Because he left a weird note."

"I'll be right over."

"I'm calling the police."

"No. Ryan, wait until I talk to Dorrie."

What if they didn't have time? He hadn't spoken out against that stunt with the tractor and Sara ended up dead. He wasn't going to ignore his gut feeling this time. He faced a no-win situation but had to act. Hesitation might make all the difference in the safety of those two little girls. No way was he risking that.

"I'm calling them, Kel."

By the time Ryan got off the phone with 911, Kellie had pulled into the driveway. He met her at the door. "Did you get a hold of Dorrie?"

Kellie shook her head as she walked inside looking scared.

He handed her the crumpled note. "The sheriff's office is sending a car to her place to be sure. I didn't know Dorrie's address, only that she lived in a mobile home the other side of a field next to Three Corner Community Church. I also told them about her Church Hammers house."

Kellie's face paled after she read her brother's cryptic letter, but she raised a defiant chin. "Karl is not violent. He wouldn't hurt those girls."

"Would he take them?" Ryan imagined all kinds of things happening, none of them good. "Call Dorrie again."

Kellie did as instructed but got the same result. "Voice mail."

Ryan heard the knock at the door and opened it to a law enforcement officer.

"Ryan Marsh? I'm Deputy Williams. Can I come in?"

"Yes, yes, please." Ryan led the deputy to the couch and tried to breathe. Worry had a way of choking off air. "This is Kellie Cavanaugh, Karl's sister. Have a seat."

"Ma'am. When was the last time either of you had contact with Karl?"

"I talked to him last night," Kellie said.

"I saw him this morning, before I left for church," Ryan answered. "There was a note on my counter when I got back. That's why I called."

"Can I see this note?"

Kellie handed it over.

The deputy read it then looked at both of them. "Is there any reason why this guy might go after his kids?"

"Their mother put the kibosh on seeing them," Ryan said. He never should have agreed to Karl volunteering there until he knew the guy better. Until he knew he could be trusted.

Kellie gave him a sharp look. "My brother has a history of drug addiction, and he's never been a father to his girls. Recently, he finished a treatment program and came here hoping to see my nieces and make amends to their mother. Karl helped out at the Church Hammer house being built for my sister-in-law."

Deputy Williams jotted down some notes. "Why did your sister-in-law stop Karl from seeing his kids?"

"Because Karl wanted the girls to know that he was their father and Dorrie didn't. She told him not to come back." Kellie's voice sounded calm, but her eyes looked wild with fear.

"And when was this?"

"Yesterday." Kellie and Ryan both answered.

The deputy looked at Ryan. "You were there, too?"

"Yeah."

"Karl seemed like he'd finally gotten his act together," Kellie said. "He was seeing a sponsor and I thought this time, he might stick around."

The deputy paused in writing. "So he's taken off before?"

"All the time," Kellie said.

Ryan watched Deputy Williams's features relax a little. Had he called the officer out on a wild-goose chase?

The deputy's two-way radio crackled to life. He picked up and nodded a few times and then clicked it off. "Your sister-in-law and her girls are fine. They're home. We're going to keep them under surveillance though."

Kellie's eyes widened. "Are you sure that's necessary? My brother's not a threat. Why would he be after all this time?"

"Hard to say ma'am."

Kellie's cell phone rang and she checked the screen. "That's Dorrie. Do you mind if I take this?"

The deputy officer nodded. "Go ahead."

Ryan watched Kellie step away from them. He heard her tell Dorrie to calm down and then she explained what was going on, that he'd called the county sheriff's office. Ryan felt like a heel. Had he freaked everyone out for nothing?

He looked at the deputy. "So, now what?"

"Give me a description of this guy and then we'll wait and see what happens."

"Do you have an email? He's in some pictures I took of construction."

The officer handed Ryan a business card. Ryan grabbed his phone and whipped off the attachment while he gave as much information as he could about Karl and the car he drove. He glanced at Kellie. She paced while she was on the phone. That nervous energy of hers was far from confident. She didn't know what to expect from her brother either.

The officer rose from the couch. "Call me if something comes up."

"Yeah, thanks." Ryan shook the deputy's hand feeling like he'd made a mountain out of molehill.

From the sounds of Kellie's conversation, Dorrie wasn't

too happy with his actions either. He prayed he was wrong, but something still chafed inside. And then his stomach turned as he remembered his trash and the meds he'd thrown away.

He looked at the deputy. "I'll walk you out. There's something I need to check before you leave, okay?"

The officer cocked his head. "What's up?"

Ryan nodded for the door. He grabbed his coat hanging on a hook and glanced at Kellie again. She didn't look like she'd end the call anytime soon.

Good.

He followed the deputy to his car. "Don't leave just yet. There's something I threw away that I hope is still there."

Deputy Williams nodded. "I'm right here filling out my report."

Ryan walked to the end of his driveway. With each step, he battled cowardice. If the meds were there, then no harm done. If they were gone, Kellie might never forgive him for turning her brother in. But who else would have taken them? The biting wind whipped cold and fierce, stinging his cheeks.

When he reached the trash can, Ryan lifted the lid and let loose a sigh. The small brown paper sack he'd used to hide the bottle of prescription pain meds lay on top. He opened the bag and noticed the bottle was still inside. He pulled it out and the screw-on top fell to the ground.

Empty.

Had the pills fallen out? Maybe he didn't tighten the lid right. Ryan dug a little deeper, past discarded coffee grounds and orange peels. Nothing.

Come on, God. Let them be here. Ryan kept digging.

"What are you looking for?" the deputy asked.

Ryan straightened, defeated. "This bottle of Percocet was full. At least, I thought it was full."

"Yours?"

Ryan nodded. He hadn't bothered to count the pills before he threw them away. If Karl had been taking them, it wouldn't take a rocket scientist to figure out where they'd gone. And Ryan's trash can was in plain sight.

He looked at the deputy. "From when I had my wisdom teeth pulled a couple months ago. I took only one pill and threw the rest away when I realized I still had them. But they're gone."

The deputy took the empty bottle. "Can I have this?"

"Sure. Take it."

The deputy stood in front of him, his face like stone. "Let's go back inside. I have a few more questions."

The rustling sound of the wind against the paper bag in his hands filled the air. Ryan didn't like the look of suspicion that grew in the deputy's eyes. Ryan couldn't prove that Karl took the pills. So, why'd the guy look at him like he was the liar here, the cheat? Had the deputy found out about his recent arrest and court order? Ryan hated being in the system. He was close to getting those charges dropped, but not close enough.

He swallowed irritation and followed the deputy back inside with a sinking feeling. Ryan had a lot to prove with this discussion, starting with his credibility.

Chapter Twelve

Kellie glanced up as Ryan came back into the house. Something was wrong if the thundercloud of his face was any indication. Apprehension pooled in her belly, turning it over like she'd eaten something bad. "Dorrie, I've got to go. Call me if you see Karl."

Stepping toward him, Kellie narrowed her gaze. "What's going on?"

Ryan's brow only furrowed deeper. "My pain meds are gone."

"What pain meds?"

"From my wisdom teeth."

Kellie remembered Ryan telling her about them during his intake assessment at LightHouse Center. She fought for control and lost. "You never threw them away?"

The deputy walked back into the house and gave her an odd look at her raised voice.

Why was he still here? Did Ryan tell him about the missing meds, too? Ryan's irresponsibility with his prescription was like hanging a carrot out for a rabbit. "How could you have left them lying around knowing Karl's history?"

Ryan ran a hand through his hair. "I forgot about them."

"Do you believe your brother took the pills?" The deputy pinned her with his steely stare.

"Yes. I imagine he probably did." Kellie had to be honest. So much for thinking the best of someone she loved. The reality was that Karl most likely took them, and that's why he left.

She paced the wood floor between the dining area and the living room as more dismal thoughts swamped her. Maybe Karl's story about treatment was nothing but a ruse to keep her happy and willing to give him money. But her brother *had* been meeting his sponsor. That hadn't been a lie; she'd checked. The only thing she knew was real was Karl's eagerness to see his girls. But he wouldn't take them, too, would he?

"So, what's next?" Ryan slid into a chair at the dining room table. He gestured for the officer to do the same.

"We'll look for him and then talk to him." The deputy focused on Ryan. "Is there anything else missing? Any other meds?"

Ryan shook his head. "All I have is aspirin and maybe a box of cold medicine."

"Can I take a look?"

"Sure."

Kellie stopped pacing and leaned against the back of the couch, chewing the edge of her thumb as she watched Ryan lead the officer to his bathroom. She listened as the two men talked in low tones while going through the cabinet. The officer asked if this was where Ryan had kept his prescription.

How could she not have seen this coming? She should have asked Ryan if he had anything that might tempt Karl. She could have made sure those pills had been properly disposed of before he had moved in. Kellie closed her eyes, soaking in the weight of her failure.

She felt a warm hand on her shoulder and looked up into Ryan's concerned eyes. "This isn't how I envisioned you taking Karl in."

Ryan gave her a wan smile. "No, I suppose not."

The deputy joined them. "Thank you both. Miss Cavanaugh, I'll call you if anything develops with your brother."

Kellie nodded as she watched Ryan walk the guy outside. Her nerves raw, she went to one of the windows and looked out at the stark landscape. Hues of brown and gray were everywhere. Brown grass, brown-and-gray trees rose up to meet a gray sky. Even the lake looked gray. Sullen.

Kellie hung her head against the cold glass. She hated being used. Yet, she'd let it happen again. This time by her own brother.

Once an addict, always an addict.

Was there no escaping that truth? Maybe she was an addict for heartbreak—always putting herself out there only to be disappointed.

"You okay?"

Kellie whirled around. "No, I'm not. And I don't think Dorrie or the girls are either. That sheriff showing up scared them all."

"You know I had to make that call." His tone was soft but firm, much like the voice she used with the second graders at school.

She stared at him. She wanted to stomp her feet and yell. He was right of course, but the helplessness running through her had given way to anger. Anger at Ryan for doing the right thing, anger at Karl for doing the wrong thing, but mostly anger at herself for doing nothing to prevent this. What kind of counselor would she make if she couldn't even get it right with her own family?

She grabbed her coat. "I'm going over there."

Ryan stopped her with a touch on her arm. "Kellie, wait. Talk to me."

"Not now. I might say something we'd both regret." She wanted to blame him so badly, she could taste it. But this wasn't his fault.

He let out a weary sigh. "Call me if you hear from Karl. And if he shows up at Dorrie's, promise you'll call the sheriff."

Kellie nodded, avoiding Ryan's gaze.

He tipped up her chin. "Promise me."

She searched his dark brown eyes for something that might resemble regret, but found only a sure resolve and a fierce protectiveness. It made her shiver.

Ryan had taken in Karl as a favor to her, and look what had happened. She had to get out of there before she broke down. "Okay, okay. I promise."

"Be careful, Kel." His voice sounded stern.

"I will." She left Ryan's house with her cell phone against her ear, calling Karl once more. "Come on, pick up."

Nothing but his voice mail.

Karl was running again, and Kellie had the sinking feeling that this time he'd get caught and it wouldn't be good. She'd do her best to watch over Dorrie and the girls, but if Karl tried something he shouldn't, she'd make that call to the police. She should never have relied on Ryan to take care of her problem—her own brother. And if the authorities were needed, it might mean the end for Karl. But at least it would be Kellie's call this time.

Later that night, Ryan drove slowly by Dorrie's house and spotted Kellie's car still in the driveway. Soft light shone from the windows of the little mobile home, and he could see the girls running around inside, safe and sound. Good.

More than anything, he wanted to knock on that door and check in, but he'd give Kellie her space. She'd been too quick to hang up with him after their clipped conversation earlier. So he'd called Dorrie this last time, only an hour or so ago, to make sure they were all safe.

Kellie took Karl's disappearance hard, personally even, as if she could have somehow saved her brother from himself. Ryan knew his pain meds disappearing didn't help matters. He'd been lax and could never make that right. Even so, why had Karl left that note? Almost as if he'd raised a red flag that screamed, *come get me*.

Ryan drove north toward Dorrie's new house to check it out. He couldn't call it a night until he'd done something, anything that might help. More like keeping his mind off Kellie. He couldn't go home, not yet.

Pulling into the drive, everything looked fine and quiet, until he spotted a small flash of light from inside. Could be one of the rechargeable tools left plugged in, but Ryan wasn't going to let it go until he made sure. Getting out of his truck, he looked around. He didn't see any cars other than the ones parked in the driveways down the road at a couple of the new builds completed a few years ago.

The eerie sound of a metal For Sale sign clanging against its post in one of the vacant lots made him pause. What was he going to do if someone was inside the house? Touching the cell phone in his coat pocket, Ryan stepped forward. He'd soon find out.

Unlocking the side door, he went in. "Hello? Anyone here?"

Not a single sound greeted him.

He walked farther into the house, through the kitchen into the dining room. Nothing. But he'd seen that flash of light come from the back—from one of the bedrooms. Stepping softly down the hall, Ryan considered the risk. He might be a big guy, but what if the intruder had a weapon? Fear skittered up his spine. If he backed off now, he might miss catching whoever may be inside.

Blowing out his breath, Ryan kept walking. His skin itched and his pulse pounded like thunder in his ears. Opening the door to the girls' bedroom, Ryan scanned the empty space. Nothing amiss. He stepped across the hall and opened the other bedroom door to a blast of cold air. The window was wide open.

He ran to it and peered out. A dark figure headed for a patch of woods. If Ryan hurried, he might catch the guy. A tall, thin guy.

"Karl, wait." Tearing out of the room, Ryan ran.

Once out the back door, he charged for those woods. He couldn't see the dark figure anymore, but he heard the start of a car. The taillights were ahead of him and he got a good look at the license plate. Memorizing the numbers and letters as he ran, Ryan almost made it to the vehicle, a dark sedan that looked uncomfortably familiar, but it suddenly pulled away fast once the guy turned on to a two-track that cut through a neighboring orchard.

Ryan stopped running and dialed 911. It had to be Karl.

"Dispatch."

"Yeah, I'd like to report an intruder. I've got a license plate for you."

"Go ahead."

Ryan rattled off the plate. "I'm pretty sure it's a Lexus sedan."

"Stay put. A deputy is in route."

Ryan braced his hands on his knees, trying to catch his breath. Why had Karl stayed around? And what was he up to hanging out at Dorrie's new place? Nothing felt right or made sense.

In the distance, he heard the sound of sirens. Had they pulled him over already? Then he saw a sheriff's car pulling into the driveway next to his truck and his heart sank. The adrenaline ebbed and realization hit. Before this night was over, he'd have to tell Kellie that he'd not only found her brother but gotten him arrested.

By the time Ryan stood on the small porch outside where Dorrie lived, he knew he'd done the right thing. But how was he supposed to convince Kellie of that? Taking a deep breath, he knocked.

Kellie opened the door. Red-rimmed green eyes that matched the color of her shirt widened with fear. "What... what is it?"

Did he look that bad? His stomach churned. Probably. "Karl has been arrested."

"When?"

"A little bit ago."

She blinked. "Why would they call you and not me?"

Ryan lowered the boom. "Because I was there. I made the call."

"Where?" Her voice was barely above a whisper.

"I went to Dorrie's house to check on it, and Karl was there, hiding out."

Kellie hung her head and rubbed her temples. "Why would he do that?"

Ryan shrugged. "I don't know, but it wasn't good."

She shook her head and backed up. "Come in out of the cold."

"Where are the girls?" Ryan didn't want to talk about Karl in front of them.

"They're in bed."

He spotted Dorrie coming down the short hallway. "What's up?"

"Karl's been arrested," Kellie said.

"No surprise there." Dorrie's scorn was tangible and bitter. "He's probably dealing again."

Kellie turned on her sister-in-law. "Why would you say that?"

"Because I found this in my car tonight." Dorrie reached into the pocket of her jeans and pulled out a wad of bills and tossed them onto the small coffee table.

Ryan picked it up and counted. "There's eight hundred dollars here."

He watched Kellie wilt onto the faded couch. "Are you sure it's from Karl?"

"He left the money and a note saying he was sorry. Who else could it be?" Dorrie slipped into a rocking chair.

Ryan looked from one woman to the other. Pain and bitter disappointment were etched into their expressions. Karl had so much to live for and yet he'd thrown his life away. He'd given himself over to sin and destruction, leaving behind a lot of hurt and heartache. Kellie and Dorrie looked like they'd been through this over and over again, yet despite all that Karl had put them through, they still loved the guy.

Kellie's cell phone rang, shattering the momentary silence.

Ryan watched her look at the screen with dismay.

"Hi, Mom," Kellie said and then grew silent. "Karl called you?"

Ryan listened to Kellie agree to meet her parents at the Leelanau County jail in the morning. He sat down on the couch next to her and felt her posture stiffen. Did she blame him for all this? He'd take responsibility for his meds but

not for the other junk the sheriff found in Karl's posses-
sion. Big-time junk. And cash.

When she finally got off the phone, he cleared his
throat. "I can take you over there."

Kellie shook her head. "Thanks, but I'd rather go alone."

Ryan glanced at Dorrie.

She got the message and bounded from the rocker. "I'll
check on the girls."

"Let me help, Kel."

Kellie looked up with big green leaky pools for eyes.
"There's nothing you can do. I should have seen this coming, but I wanted to believe in his recovery. I wanted him
to be well."

"You couldn't have known." Ryan pulled her into his
arms.

She didn't resist and rested her head against his chest.
"But I'm trained to know. I spent months at outpatient,
enough to know that once an addict, always an addict."

Ryan pushed her back so he could see her face. He hated
hearing the defeat in her voice. "But we *can* live sober.
Don't forget that part. People make choices. One of them
is letting God heal their addiction. Heal their pain. You
have to know that or what's the point?"

She sniffed and pulled away. "Yeah, what's the point?"

He squeezed her hand. "I know it hurts, but you can't
stop believing in the process or the people you've helped.
You've helped me."

Her eyes got all watery again, and tears spilled over and
down her cheeks. "Every time I give someone a chance, I
get kicked in the teeth."

Ryan didn't know what it was like to have a loved
one with a substance abuse problem. He only knew that he
might have traveled farther down that road if Kellie
hadn't recommended him for treatment. He could have

been someone who would have hurt his friends and family. He didn't want to do that. Not for the world. Not after seeing the consequences from both group and Karl. Not after meeting Kellie, a woman who gave him every reason to want a real life again.

He caressed her cheek. "I won't ever kick you in the teeth, I promise."

She closed her eyes and more tears leaked out.

He kissed each eyelid, knowing he'd have a job ahead proving it to her. Could she find any trust in her heart left for him?

The next morning, Kellie sat across from her brother in the county jail, but he wouldn't look her in the eye. "Mom and Dad are on their way."

Karl nodded.

"Why didn't you call me? We could have worked this out." Kellie might have convinced him to return Ryan's pills, and even what was left of the old prescription he'd stolen from her landlady. But he'd never given her a chance.

"I've got a prior in Illinois and a bench warrant for not appearing in court. There's no working it out." Then he shrugged. "Doesn't matter."

She swallowed her urge to defend him, to cry out that it did matter, that *he* mattered. Her brother was going to jail, probably for a while, and that truth made her sick. "It matters to me. I want to help you. Ryan wants to help you."

Karl slouched farther in the chair. "No one can help me."

She tried to remember what Ryan had said to her last night, but fear for her brother who'd lost all hope turned her cold and clouded her memory. "Don't say that, Karl. Not when there's a God."

His lip curled into a sneer. "Yeah, right. God? Where's He been? Huh? Why'd He let me get here?"

Kellie bristled. "You put yourself here."

Her brother laughed. "Everything's black and white with you. It's a rhetorical question, Kel."

"Yeah? Well, maybe you'll finally find Him where you're going. Rhetorically speaking." Kellie didn't bother to soften her tone.

This time Karl looked right at her with stark desolation in his eyes. "There's no God where I've been, so why would He bother showing up where I'm going?"

Guilt swamped her, and fear, but also confusion. She couldn't shut up, not yet. "Why, Karl? Why did you take this road?"

He looked away. "I felt important, like I finally mattered, and that's what gets you hooked."

Kellie had no idea her brother had been as starved for attention and validation as she was growing up. "You matter. You always mattered, way more than—"

"Than you?" Karl smiled. "Is that how you saw it? I guess considering the trouble I was always in, it might have appeared that way. Mom and Dad were clueless, but they loved you best. You never let them down."

Kellie grabbed a box of tissues sitting on the table. She wiped her burning eyes and then blew her nose. But she had let them down, in quiet ways with razors and boys, and each one had torn pieces of her heart out. "We're a sorry pair."

Karl gave her a crooked smile, reminding her of the way he used to be. The brother that had at one time watched out for her and let her tag along with him and his friends. "Keep an eye on Dorrie and the girls for me, okay? I know I've never been there for them. Something I'll regret forever."

Kellie nodded. "Is that why you came here?"

"Yeah. I knew I was toast, so what was the point of showing up in court? I had to see those girls one last time. They'll be grown by the time I'm out."

Kellie's eyes widened. "You don't know that."

"I deal as well as use, Kel. And I got caught in Michigan—a state with some of the toughest penalties. I'm going away for a good long while."

Her heart ached, but part of her wanted to pound on him, too, for putting himself in this position. For putting her here. He'd had so many chances to turn his life around, but he'd blown every one of them to bits.

Karl's slouch became more pronounced and his expression changed to indifference.

Kellie looked around and her insides tightened. Their parents walked toward them.

"We've called a good lawyer. He'll be here shortly, so keep your mouth shut about what the cops found on you." Her father was a proud man with a belligerent stance. Self-made, too, until his business took a hit with the downturn of the economy. Money was tighter than it used to be, but they'd still shell out the best for Karl. Or was it more for their own benefit?

There were no hellos, or inquiries into how she or Karl might be holding up. But then, her folks had been through a lot with her brother over the years. Karl was a dark stain on the gleaming Cavanaugh reputation. He'd been arrested in their home state, and it would no doubt make the news. It didn't matter that Karl had been arrested three hours north of where they'd grown up. People back home would know. They'd find out.

Kellie wiped her eyes again and stood. "Hey, Mom and Dad."

"Oh Kellie, how'd this happen?" Her mother's eyes teared up, but accusation rang in her voice.

"You'll have to talk to Karl." Kellie wasn't about to explain Ryan's part in her brother's arrest. She wouldn't be the one to drop the bomb of a prior arrest either. Maybe her folks already knew.

"I'm asking you. You're the one who's trained in this kind of thing. Couldn't you keep him away from the drugs?"

She'd rather be kicked in the stomach; it would have hurt less. "Karl's a grown man. He made a choice."

Kellie took a seat farther down the table, letting her parents grill Karl for information. Every now and then he'd glance her way and smirk. They'd been through this before, but never this serious.

By the time the lawyer arrived, Kellie had already made herself invisible. There was nothing she could do, nothing to add, no difference to make. Was she kidding herself to think she'd be a good counselor? Ryan had told her otherwise, but could she believe him?

Her heart twisted and her mind clicked back to the day she'd taken Ryan's court-ordered assessment. Had he really been telling the truth that he'd never drink and drive? What if that story about his friend had been a lie? Would Ryan have driven home drunk that night if the cops hadn't intervened? The thought made her ill. But the possibility was all too real. What if someday it was Ryan sitting at this table?

Looking around, Kellie felt numb. Removed even, like she was watching a cheesy TV cop show. Only this was all too real, and this was her family. She'd been kicked in the teeth enough for one lifetime; no way would she allow herself to go through more. She refused to end up like her sister-in-law who'd fallen in love with the wrong man. A man who still hurt her.

Ryan had good intentions. He was a good man, but Kellie knew that good men fell, too. She wasn't sure she could be a safety net for Ryan if it might mean this kind of heartbreak. This kind of future.

Chapter Thirteen

After the meeting with Karl and the lawyer, Kellie went to lunch with her folks in Traverse City near the hotel where they'd checked in for a few days. And then she stopped at the school where she'd soon work. The principal had been pleased by her proactive visit and had directed Kellie to the office she'd occupy as well as case files she should get acquainted with before her start date. Kellie copied the files of the kids who needed the most attention and took them home to study.

She needed to get a handle on what to expect after Thanksgiving. She needed something to keep her mind occupied and off her family.

It was late by the time Kellie made it to Dorrie's new house. Entering through the side door into the laundry room that lacked only the hookup of a washer and dryer to be complete, Kellie stepped into the kitchen where everyone ate dinner.

"Perfect timing." Ryan stood and offered his chair. "Have a seat."

Kellie feasted on the sight of him. Wearing his usual plaid flannel over a thermal undershirt, Ryan might as well be the poster child of dependability. Strong and stable.

But for how long?

Making her way toward him, she nearly stumbled when she spotted her parents. She glanced at Dorrie. Her sister-in-law's eyes looked red-rimmed like she'd been crying. No doubt her folks had filled Dorrie in on what Karl faced.

"You okay?" Ryan touched her shoulder and squeezed.

"Yeah, sure." Kellie had switched into autopilot. She gathered up today's hurt and tucked it away like she'd done a dozen times before. "I just came from the school where I'll be working. I have a lot of paperwork to get familiar with."

Ryan looked at her closely. "I'm sorry about Karl."

Kellie shrugged and glanced away. "Me, too."

"Have you eaten? I'm grabbing seconds. Can I get a plate for you?"

Kellie didn't have much of an appetite, and she wasn't up for talking about her day, acting like everything was normal when it wasn't. Didn't matter that she was the one who'd already set this tone. "No, thanks. I had a late lunch. I think I'll look around a bit while you finish."

Ryan narrowed his gaze. "You sure?"

She nodded and walked away through the house and ended up in the girls' bedroom. Kellie leaned against the window seat that Ryan had made. She stared out the window at the bare cherry trees across the street and marveled at how far the house had come because of how much Ryan had done. He was a good man. Dorrie and the girls would move in before the holidays. Talk about the perfect Christmas present. All because of Ryan's commitment to hard work.

"Pretty house." Her mom stood beside her.

"Yeah." She rubbed her arms. It felt chilly inside even with the heat on.

"Karl said he'd worked on it a little bit with your boyfriend. We met Ryan when we came in. He's very nice, Kellie."

"He's not my boyfriend, Mom." A tug of regret pierced her. He could be, if she'd let him. "He's a friend. Just a friend."

"Karl spoke highly of him."

She wondered if her brother still thought that after learning Ryan had called the sheriff. But then Ryan was trying to protect Dorrie and the girls. And her. Surely, Karl understood that. "When did Karl say all this?"

"Today, after you'd left."

"Oh." Warm surprise spread through her. And then it turned cold. She still worried over her brother's opinion.

"Don't you care for Ryan?"

"Mom, this really isn't the place." Kellie's throat threatened to close up.

Care was an understatement for the feelings that spread deep and wide like an open chasm in front of her. If she took another step forward, she'd be swallowed whole and there'd be no turning back. No protection.

"Why don't you and Dorrie and the girls come home for Thanksgiving. Get away from here for a couple of days." Her mom's eyes pleaded.

Today had been hard on her mom, too. Seeing Karl and knowing where he was headed had to break a mother's heart. It still broke Dorrie's. And it broke hers, too. "Yeah, maybe."

Her mom's eyes clouded with tears as she reached out and squeezed Kellie's arm. "Let me know. I better get your father and go before he eats all the desserts."

Kellie nodded, feeling her eyes sting. She remained where she was though, unable to move as she listened to her nieces say their goodbyes to Grandma and Grandpa. The girls asked if they'd come back again tomorrow, and

Kellie's heart pinched a little tighter. There'd been sweet times in her family, so why had it gone so wrong?

Kellie heard sounds of the volunteer workers getting back to work, but she couldn't make her feet move or pull her gaze away from the window as she watched her parents climb into their car. They looked so weary and defeated.

All because of Karl. So much heartache and moments lost because of an addiction.

"Hey. Are you okay?" Ryan's voice sounded soft and deep behind her.

She shrugged. "I don't think I can work tonight."

"I imagine not. Do you want to go somewhere and talk about it?"

Kellie shook her head. "No."

He put his arm around her shoulders. "Believe it or not, I'm a good listener."

Kellie battled the temptation to lean into him and pour her heart out. Something about Ryan's embrace made her feel safe, like the rest of world couldn't touch her. But she'd followed that kind of false security too many times.

She looked into his eyes instead. "I better tell Dorrie I'm leaving."

"Don't sweat it. I'll let her know. Come on, I'll walk you out." He took her hand, the one he'd so gently bandaged. Her palm had pretty much healed.

She followed him outside, grabbing her coat and shrugging into it along the way.

At her car, Ryan gently pulled her into his arms.

And she crumpled inside. "I'm so sorry."

"For what?" He kissed the top of her head.

"For putting you through this with Karl."

He squeezed a little tighter. "I offered. It was my decision to make. I'm only sorry I was the one to turn him in."

"Yeah, me, too."

He stepped back and tipped up her chin. His eyes looked guarded and unsure. "Does that change things between us?"

Kellie could jump on that excuse, but it'd be false. Ryan had done the right thing. She needed to do the same, so she took a deep breath. "Look, Ryan…"

"That doesn't sound too good." His half smile made her heart pinch with regret.

She pulled away from him. "There can't be an *us*. At least, not for me."

He narrowed his gaze. "Why?"

How did a person explain what it was like to take a trip to jail to see a loved one? "I just can't do this anymore."

"Do what?"

"Substance abuse." She felt Ryan's stance change.

His body tightened in invasive defense. And why wouldn't he feel invaded? She'd taken an inventory of him and called him out, maybe unfairly, when he was trying to get it right. He'd been honest in group, and he'd been honest with her, too, but Kellie couldn't afford any more tries that ended in failure.

"I'm not your brother. I'm not messing around with alcohol because I know where it could lead. I won't go there. Ever."

She looked into his eyes and read genuine conviction. He had good intentions but no track record. "It's too much for me to risk."

"I'm not letting you go—"

"This isn't going to work. I can't make it work." Her voice went a little shrill.

"Says who? We haven't even gone on a date yet, and you're throwing in the towel? Give us a chance. Give *me* a chance to prove I'm someone you can trust." He took her hand. "Trust me, Kellie."

She wanted to, but how? Trust was the hardest gift to give. Her eyes burned and panic set in as she sought for an excuse to turn him away. "You're not even over your dead fiancée."

Anger flashed in his eyes at the cheap shot. "And you're afraid of something you can't control."

Like a punch to stomach, Kellie gasped. "That's not fair."

"Maybe not, but Kellie, you're so afraid of what I might do that you're not seeing straight. We're building something beautiful here, why throw it away?"

She shook her head. "I've got to go. It's cold out here and you're not wearing a coat."

"I don't care about a coat," he snapped and stepped closer. "When Sara died in my arms, she said something that has haunted me for three years."

Kellie closed her eyes. She wanted to cover her ears from hearing. She didn't want to hurt anymore but couldn't walk away. Couldn't help but ask, "What…what did she say?"

He touched a lock of her hair and twined it around his finger like he'd done so many times before, before looking into her eyes. "She said, *Don't die on me, Ryan.* All this time, I thought she was begging me not to let her die. I had let her down and that ate away at me no matter what I did. But Sunday, in church, I realized the truth for the first time. Sara wasn't afraid of death. She knew where she was going. Her fear was for me. Sara didn't want *me* to stop living. And I had, Kel. I really had died inside."

Kellie sniffed as tears trickled down her cheeks.

"Look at me," he said.

She did.

"You helped bring me back to life. Sara will always be part of who I am, but you're part of who I want to be. Don't you see? I want you in my life. I want to build a life with you. Sure, I'll let you down, but not in the ways you fear. The consequences of that slippery slope are far too steep."

His words sounded so sweet and full of promise, like a tantalizing balm to heal her wounds. But the image of meeting him at LightHouse Center flashed through her mind. The reality of how often good men and women repeated their mistakes crushed her hope. How could she be sure he wouldn't end up back in that place or worse?

"What good is this life if we don't risk loving each other? Don't let this die. Not now, not like this."

She let out the breath she'd been holding. "I can't."

"Yes, you can. Open your heart and trust in the God we try to serve."

God. The only one who wouldn't let her down, but did she really believe that? Or was it her own ability to keep her heart safe that she relied upon? No matter how much she trusted God, Ryan had the power to shatter her world.

Kellie looked at him, so solid and real. A good man. Could God keep him from drinking? Not if Ryan chose otherwise.

Snow started falling from the sky. Beautiful fat flakes of white promising to cover the ground with its purity. But even snow eventually got dirty.

She reached up and caressed his face, while the weight of what she might be throwing away suffocated her. "I'm sorry."

"I'm sorry, too." His eyes clouded over with sadness and regret.

"Goodbye, Ryan." Kellie climbed in behind the wheel and started her car before she changed her mind.

Ryan watched her drive away. He couldn't blame her for how afraid she felt. Standing alone in the cold, he prayed that somehow God would make her believe him. Believe in him enough to come back. He ran his hand through hair that was wet from the gigantic snowflakes and returned to the house.

He spotted Dorrie's girls with their noses pressed against the window watching the snow silently blanket the ground. Several volunteers chatted about how good the snow would be for the opening of deer season later that week. He'd lose a lot of help then, but they were close to being done with the house anyway. He'd help the builder in charge do the finishing touches before ordering the occupancy permit and then he'd be done, too.

His community service hours had already been satisfied, and once he finished his treatment, the charges against him would be dropped and the stain of this entire incident would be sponged away. Or would it? What if Kellie was right and he couldn't keep that promise he'd made?

A touch on his shoulder startled him.

"Where's Kellie?" Dorrie asked.

He cleared his throat. "She went home."

Dorrie's eyes narrowed. "And you look like you lost your last friend. Did you two have a fight?"

Ryan shook his head. "She's taking what happened to Karl pretty hard."

"She's not blaming you for—"

"No." Ryan shrugged. "She's scared, Dorrie. Too scared to take a chance with me."

Dorrie nodded, her expression soft with understanding. "It's not easy for her to be vulnerable. She's fought against that her whole life."

"But she can trust me." *God, please help me to make it so.*

"Where we've been, trust doesn't come easy." Dorrie spoke from experience.

From what Ryan had gathered, she'd tried with Karl and had her heart crushed one too many times. But he wasn't Karl. He knew what he had. What he'd been blessed with. Would Kellie ever love him enough to overcome her fears? That was a question only she could answer. And he could do nothing but wait it out.

It was late by the time Ryan left Dorrie's for home. His heart felt heavy and it hurt. Working on Dorrie's house reminded him of time spent with Kellie. Everywhere he looked, Kellie was there. That heaviness settled inside his soul and made him feel empty and lost all over again.

He spotted the mini-mart on the corner and part of him wanted to stop and grab a six-pack. His thoughts justified the need to relax, but he knew better. He wanted to forget his feelings again, numb them, even if for a night. But he'd need more than a six-pack to do that.

He kept driving instead. And he prayed, like he'd never done before.

After pulling into his driveway, Ryan stared at his darkened house on the lake with bitter resolve. He wanted to curse and yell but knew it wouldn't get him anywhere. He was tired of being alone. He wanted to be married. He wanted a wife. He wanted Kellie.

Once inside, he flicked on the light switch and glanced at his cell phone for what felt like the hundredth time, hoping for a message from Kellie. Nothing. He slouched into his chair and clicked on the TV, not bothering to build a fire. That trip to the mini-mart called out to him again, only a little stronger this time.

Ryan closed his eyes. He had to face the fact that the reason he'd gotten drunk that night at the party was because the effect of having a few beers every night had worn off. They hadn't quite eased the pain then, and they wouldn't now. And if he got drunk again, could he ever face what he'd become? He'd lose the battle, and that would cost him any chance he might still have with Kellie.

Oh, but the emptiness remained like a bottomless pit, despite what his brain told him. What he knew inside as true. He checked his watch. Too late to call his counselor at LightHouse Center. He'd see him tomorrow at group anyway.

Restlessness coursed through him, so he got up and looked out the window. Snow still fell, blanketing the ground in patches of white. They'd have a good couple of inches or more by morning. He could split wood, but it was too late and quiet; he didn't want the sound to echo and bother his neighbors.

"God," he breathed. "I hate this hollow feeling. Please take the craving from me. Please, God."

He sat back down and hung his head in his hands for a few moments before he picked up his cell phone and scrolled the contact list. Without hesitating, he hit the button to connect and waited.

"Hello?" Sinclair's voice sounded sleepy.

"Sin?" Ryan's voice cracked.

"What's wrong?"

"I'm struggling here. Talk to me for a bit, will you?"

After the briefest of pauses, his brother said, "Hang tight. I'll be right over."

Ryan set down his phone, and his body went limp. This is what Kellie was afraid of. What she'd always fear with him. He couldn't say that he blamed her, because he didn't have it conquered like he thought. And that scared him, too.

"Pass the gravy, please?" Kellie's mom smiled.

Kellie handed it over after dousing her mound of

mashed potatoes. Thanksgiving dinner was her favorite meal, but she couldn't rouse the appetite to eat much of it.

It'd been over a week since that awful conversation with Ryan. He hadn't called her, hadn't shown up under her window with a handful of pebbles like she'd hoped. Her resolve might have caved if he had. Didn't he realize that?

"When can we have pie?" Gracie asked.

She grinned at her niece. Despite her loss of appetite, Kellie might make an exception for a piece of cherry crumb pie. "That's up to your mom and Grandma."

The girls had loved helping make pies the day before. All five Cavanaugh women had worked side by side in the kitchen, and Kellie had to admit the smell of home and holidays had lightened her mood. But she hadn't once forgotten the ache she carried inside, like a cast-iron anchor that was too big for the boat and dragged her down.

"After we eat dinner," Dorrie said.

Hannah played with her food. "Will Karl have Thanksgiving dinner in jail?"

A hush settled over the festive table that had been decorated with a pair of pilgrim candlesticks on either side of a rust-colored floral centerpiece of mums and carnations.

Kellie glanced at her parents. Sadness lurked in their eyes, and both of their shoulders seemed to slump. It wasn't hard to imagine Karl all alone today.

"I'm sure he'll have something good to eat," Dorrie said with a voice more cheerful than she probably felt. "Now finish up your plate, Hannah."

"Excuse me. I forgot something in the kitchen." Kellie's mom got up from the table.

Kellie looked at her dad. Would he go after her? When he didn't, she got up instead. Stepping softly into the kitchen, she spotted her mother at the sink holding a dishtowel to her face. "Mom?"

"I'm sorry," her mom sniffed.

"It's okay. This is hard on everyone."

Her mother turned to face her. Her eyes watered and her nose looked red. "If only I would have done things differently."

Kellie cocked her head. "What do you mean?"

"We left you kids alone too much. And when we were home, we were preoccupied with that stupid business." Her mother pointed toward the dining room. "He still hides at the office far too much."

Kellie had never heard her mother speak poorly of their real estate business before. Despite the long hours and weekends their business demanded, it had always been the source of their pride. Their passion. Their kids, not so much. "I thought you loved what you did."

Her mom sighed. "I did. I do. But we were too wrapped up in it and we forgot what was truly important. We forgot about our kids. Karl suffered, and I think you did, too."

Kellie's eyes went wide. When had her mother come to this realization? "Why say all this now?"

Her mother shrugged. "Because I'm seeing a counselor. I'm trying to come to terms with what I did or didn't do to make Karl turn out like he has."

Kellie's heart twisted. "Oh Mom, Karl made his own choices."

"And what about you? You're so distant and in control. Kellie, I fear you're turning into stone. Strong, but cold."

She took a step back, shaken by her mother's perception. "I'm okay."

"Are you? Are you really?" Her mother gave her a sad look before grabbing the dish of cranberry sauce that had been left behind.

Kellie followed her back to the dining room table, contemplating her mother's words, stunned by their truth. Was it so bad to be in control? Exchanging a look with Dorrie, Kellie refused to answer and got back to the business of eating what she could.

They finished their meal in silence, and then cleanup wasn't much better. There was only so much small talk to be said. Pie was served in the living room while a fire roared in the hearth and her father watched the Lions play football on TV. Picking at her piece of cherry crumb pie, Kellie kept thinking about Ryan. His family grew cherries. She'd never been to their farm but could easily imagine how beautiful it'd look when the cherry blossoms were in bloom. Ryan had promised to show her.

Too many thoughts turned to him.

When she finally slid into the bed she shared with Dorrie, Kellie stared at the walls of her old room plastered with her high school cheerleading memorabilia and girlish decorations. She'd saved a meaningless corsage she'd worn to her senior prom. What a joke that had been. Her date hadn't cared about her, and yet Kellie had clung to misplaced hope that he would.

Kellie sighed, drained.

"Ryan's nothing like Karl, you know." Dorrie fluffed her pillow.

"I know."

"I'm not so sure you do. Think about it. Ryan's had what, one girlfriend in high school, and he would have married her if she hadn't died. If that isn't proof of commitment, I don't know what is."

"This isn't about his commitment to me."

"Isn't it? Don't you think he'll be just as committed to his recovery?"

Kellie's eyes went wide. Ryan had said that he got done what he set out to do. Dorrie's house was certainly proof of that.

"He told me about why he needed community service hours. He also told me that he never had issues with drinking until recently. Don't you see? Ryan faced his problem. Karl never faced anything about himself. It was always everyone else's fault—your parents, his coaches, his boss. He was irresponsible and lacked commitment from the get-go only I was too stupid to see it."

Kellie settled her head deeper into her pillow, while she weighed Dorrie's words. "But what if—"

"Life's full of what-ifs. You're a counselor now. Do you believe all that you learned is false?"

"No, of course not."

"Then why can't you believe in Ryan? He's gotten help and is putting into practice what he's learned. He loves you, Kellie, what more do you want?"

"A guarantee." The words slipped out, and hearing them, Kellie realized how crazy they sounded.

"Well, good luck. There isn't anyone who can give you that. Even God doesn't guarantee that life will be easy. He only promises never to leave us."

Kellie opened her mouth and then shut it. She didn't have an argument for that one. She pulled the covers up under her chin and felt the old scars on her arms. Maybe she'd turned to stone because a hunk of rock didn't need to bleed. Didn't need to feel. Didn't need to believe.

That Bible verse in Corinthians came back to taunt her—*Love never gives up, never loses faith...*

She hadn't even given Ryan a chance. She'd condemned him to failure because she was scared.

"He's a good man, Kellie." Dorrie gave her shoulder a squeeze before rolling over.

"I know." But did she really?

Kellie lay awake long after Dorrie had dozed off. Listening to her sister-in-law's even breathing, she watched the moon shadows dance across her ceiling. Dorrie was right. She didn't believe in Ryan. What did that say about her as a counselor, and even worse, as a Christian?

Anything she had to say to these kids she'd soon meet and serve would be nothing but empty words if she didn't believe people could face their weaknesses and change. Didn't her mother prove that was possible tonight? Her mom had finally faced their past and was trying to deal with it.

Kellie had no right to give kids advice she couldn't even follow. She was a sham—a stone who'd let her heart grow cold with fear. She might as well not show up for work Monday morning.

Kellie closed her eyes and prayed. "Please Lord, help me to believe."

Chapter Fourteen

"Are you sure your brother got the message?" Kellie peered out the window of her office. The lines of yellow buses had long since pulled away from the school's curb.

"He'll be here. He had band practice." Destiny, one of her sixth graders, tossed her shoulder-length blond hair while her fingers tapped away on her cell phone.

"Our mom called you, right?" Her brother Kevin was a couple of years older and a serious kid. He questioned every rule, and tested them.

Even so, Kellie had to resist the urge to ruffle the boy's hair every time she saw him. "Yes. She asked if you both could wait with me until Kenneth picked you up."

Kellie made an attempt to clean off her desk while the kids waited. Too many papers and files had stacked up this week, and she was behind schedule. But then she was still learning the ropes, probably would be for the next couple of years.

"Are you going to the dance tomorrow night?" Kevin asked.

"I'm chaperoning."

"Ooohh good," Destiny piped up from her texting. "Kenneth's band is playing and they're really good."

"Ah yes, the Mealy Peaches." Kellie suppressed a laugh. "I've heard that, too."

Their oldest brother played bass in a high school band, and tomorrow night's dance was their shining debut. Kellie had no idea what style of music was their specialty, but with a name like Mealy Peaches, their sound had to be a little quirky.

"You got a date?" Kevin asked.

"I'll know tonight." Kellie smiled as she filed folders in her credenza.

Tonight, Dorrie was hosting a Christmas Open House in her new home. All the Church Hammer volunteers had been invited, and no doubt Ryan would be there, too. Her heart flipped thinking about it.

"You kids ready?" Kenneth poked his head through the open door of her office. "Thanks, Miss Cavanaugh, for watching them."

"You're welcome."

Both younger siblings gave him a dirty look like they didn't need a babysitter, only a place to wait for him.

"If you're going to the dance tomorrow, save one for me." Kenneth winked at her.

The kid had too much charm for his own good, and Kellie laughed. "I'm pretty sure my date wouldn't approve."

"Who are you going to ask, Miss Cavanaugh? Mr. Smith?" Destiny shouldered her backpack and pocketed her cell phone.

Mr. Smith was the math teacher and also single. "No. I'm hoping a friend of mine will go with me."

"Well, I think he'll say yes if he knows what's good for him." Destiny gave her a big sweet smile. The girl meant what she said.

Kellie smiled back. "Thank you. I hope so."

She waved goodbye to the kids who'd become her favorite students. She hoped Ryan would accept her invitation. She also hoped he'd understand what the asking meant. She wanted another shot at building a relationship with him. She wanted a second chance, and she prayed he'd want that, too.

Ryan mingled with people he'd spent the last couple of months working with to get Dorrie's house finished. The place looked nice decorated for Christmas and smelled even better with the balsam scent of a freshly cut tree. Instrumental Christmas music played softly in the background while snow fell outside. Her house felt like a real home complete with the sounds of kids laughing while they played a board game in the bedroom.

That hollow feeling struck quick and sharp. His house didn't feel like a home, only a place to live. And this holiday season felt more lonesome than ever. He grabbed a cup of citrus punch and glanced at the doorway. Would Kellie stay away tonight because of him? He hoped not.

She'd stopped coming to work on the house after that night. Not that there was that much left to do. And he'd only exchanged a few words with her since then—an awkward hello at church and then some silly moving jokes while packing up Dorrie and her girls a couple of weeks ago. He missed her.

Sinclair slapped him on the back. "She'll show."

"I hope so." He wanted to talk to her. Needed to, in fact.

After eating a couple of the small fancy sandwiches laid out on decorative plates, Ryan looked up exactly when Kellie entered the kitchen through the laundry room. He swallowed the last of his punch pretty hard.

He'd never before seen her look so pretty. She wore a plaid wool skirt over tights and a navy turtleneck sweater that hugged her slender form. She'd left her hair loose in a riot of curls. He openly stared. Probably drooled, too.

Her cheeks were rosy pink, but then she'd just come in from the cold. Without hesitation, she walked straight for him and smiled. She didn't look inclined to avoid him this time.

His heart rate picked up speed.

"Hi, Ryan." Her voice sounded rich as silk.

"You look beautiful," he blurted.

"Thanks." She gave him a quick once-over. Bold as can be. "So do you."

What was she doing to him? He quickly changed the subject to keep from pulling her into his arms. "How's school counseling?"

Her eyes brightened. They looked steely blue tonight, almost gray. "I love it."

He shoved his hands in the pockets of his khakis to keep from touching her. "That's good. I'm glad."

"How are you?" Her eyes narrowed. "I mean really."

"I finished group. John signed off on my master treatment plan. Everything's been sent to the court to drop the charges."

"That's good. I'm glad," she echoed his words.

"But I'm not done, Kel." He took a deep breath and held it, waiting for her reaction. This is what he'd wanted to tell her, hoping she'd come tonight.

Her eyebrow lifted.

He stepped closer. "I'm going to AA meetings once a week."

"Really?" Her eyes widened in surprise.

He caught his brother's eye from across the room and Sinclair gave him a nod. His brother had come through for him when he'd needed him most. Sinclair had made him see that there was no shame in seeking help. No shame in admitting what he'd become.

Ryan came clean. "They say *once an alcoholic always, an alcoholic but we can live sober.* I plan on living sober."

He watched her eyes fill with tears and panicked. Not the reaction he'd hoped for. "It's a good thing, Kel. Really."

"I know."

"Then why are you crying?"

She sniffed and then laughed. "I guess I'm not made of stone, after all."

"I never thought you were." Ryan caught one of her tears with his thumb. No way. She was warm and caring and kissed with fire. "I never thought you were."

Kellie's eyes softened even more. "Karl said that you'd been to see him."

"I had to see him. And we're keeping in touch." He'd made his peace with *her* brother, too.

"I really appreciate that. Karl does, too." She gave him another watery smile and he feared she might start crying again.

"I missed you," he whispered.

"And I missed you." Her voice sounded raw.

"So, what should we do about it?"

Kellie pulled out a tissue from her pocket and blew her nose into it. "Sorry."

He chuckled. "No problem. Want to get a plate of food and sit down somewhere?"

She shook her head. "Not yet. I wonder if you'd consider…"

He watched her rally her courage and waited for her to continue.

"Would you be willing to go with me to a middle school dance tomorrow night?"

He laughed. "Are you a chaperone?"

She straightened her shoulders. "Yes, I am."

He leaned a little closer. "I'd love to go."

"Then it's a date. Pick me up at six-thirty?" She crinkled her nose.

Ryan smiled. He would not have envisioned a middle school dance as their first date, but he'd take it. It was a start of many dates. "You'll dance with me?"

Her cheeks colored. "Uh yeah, it's a dance."

He suddenly couldn't wait for tomorrow night to hold her. He lowered his voice and asked, "Why don't we go somewhere for hot chocolate and talk about it."

Kellie's eyes widened again. "But I haven't said hello to anyone. Not even Dorrie."

"Meet me at my truck in thirty minutes."

She opened her mouth and then closed it and nodded.

Ryan couldn't believe she didn't argue, and that made him smile. He imagined that they'd argue over many things, but that meant they'd make up, too. After she walked away to mingle, he checked his watch. This was going to be the longest half hour of his life.

Kellie made a dash for Ryan's truck. Her heart skittered and clanged against her ribs while she waited. Was she too early? She hadn't kept track of time. And then she saw him and her insides flipped.

Ryan jogged toward her, his breath blowing white in front him. "Sorry," he said. "Were you waiting long?"

She looked up at his dear face with those bittersweet chocolate eyes. Snowflakes clung to his dark hair and she fluffed them away with her fingertips. He was the gallant knight of her girlish dreams and he'd slayed a couple of dragons belonging to him and her. "I've been waiting my whole life for you."

"That's good to hear." He wrapped his arms around her

and pulled her close. "I won't fail you, Kellie. I'm in this for the long haul. God's got my back and I'm not afraid."

"I'm not either." She really meant it, too. "And Ryan?"

"Yeah?"

She licked her lips. "I love you, and I believe in you. I believe in us."

"I need your love, Kel. Trust can come later after I've earned it. I will, too. By God's grace, I'll earn it."

She didn't bother reminding him that trust was something she needed to give. She'd prove it to him with time and the life they'd build together. "You can start by sealing that promise with a kiss."

"Gladly." He dipped his head and captured her mouth with his.

She returned his kiss with a promise of her own running through her mind and soul. *To have and to hold, in sickness and in health...*

No matter what their future held, God would be with them.

When they finally broke apart, Ryan cupped her face. "I love you, Kellie Cavanaugh."

She gave him a cheeky grin. "I know."

He laughed and shook his head while he opened the door for her. "Now, get in the truck."

She climbed in and scooted close to Ryan, breathing in the frosty air and luscious scent of him. "This is where it all started, huh? The night my car broke down and you picked me up."

He reached across her for the middle seat belt and buckled her in place right next to him. "I think it started the moment you shook my hand. I knew there was something special about you."

Kellie nodded. "I remember feeling the same way about you, and it scared me to pieces."

"Thank you." He cupped her cheek and gave her a smile that made her toes curl inside her boots.

She tipped her head. "For what?"

"For making a difference."

Kellie felt her eyes sting again and her throat clog with emotion. She pulled Ryan's head toward hers and showed him the difference he'd made with a kiss.

Trust in God was the real difference, though. Maybe the Hound of Heaven had tracked them both down and thrown them together to help each other heal. To help each other grow and find redemptive love that would last forever.

Epilogue

A light snow fell as a local band played a Kid Rock song that had become something of an anthem in Northern Michigan. Gathered near the gigantic Christmas tree on Front Street in Traverse City, the entire crowd joined in singing. Kellie sang, too.

Ryan glanced at her and smiled.

"What?"

"I love hearing you sing."

Kellie laughed. She practically screamed the words, but whatever.

They'd been dating ever since Dorrie's open house. They'd spent the Christmas holidays visiting both his and her parents and now, here they were with Dorrie and her girls celebrating New Year's Eve.

Ryan bounced Gracie on his shoulders to the music and she laughed. Her breath made little white puffs in the cold air.

At the conclusion of the song, the announcer shouted out to get ready for the cherry to drop. Cheers went up and then the crowd chanted the number countdown as the red ball of lights made its descent.

Ten.

Nine.

Kellie glanced at Ryan. He was yelling the numbers out, too, right along with Gracie. He was so good with Dorrie's girls. Warmth spread through Kellie at the thought he'd make a good father. Ryan was good with her, too. He was patient and easy and she could tell him anything. She closed her eyes and thanked God for bringing them together. To think she'd almost tossed away this chance at happiness.

Five.

Four.

And then Ryan put Gracie on her feet and nodded. The kid grinned then pushed past her toward Dorrie.

Kellie tipped her head, ready to ask why he'd done that, but it was time.

Two.

One.

The crowd cheered "Happy New Year," and folks hugged each other as fireworks burst to life overhead with crackles and booms. Ryan reached for her mitten-clad hands.

"Kellie?" He looked very serious and then went down on one knee.

Kellie's breath caught in her throat. "Oh."

The crowd around them inched away, giving Ryan room. A couple of folks poked each other with elbows and watched. Kellie glanced at Dorrie, who smiled and wiped at a tear.

Slowly, as if in a dream, Kellie focused her attention back on Ryan kneeling in the icy street.

"I promised to wait, but since it's a new year, I thought it'd be okay to finally ask if you'll marry me."

Kellie laughed. They hadn't been dating three weeks. Three weeks or three years, her answer would remain the same. "Yes! Yes! Now get up before you freeze."

He stood and pulled her into his arms. "Happy New Year, Kel."

She lifted her face. "Happy New Year."

He kissed her then, sealing their promise.

She felt a hug from someone small. Breaking apart from Ryan, Kellie looked down to see Gracie grinning up at them. "You knew, didn't you?"

"Yup." Gracie nodded.

"And she didn't tell. That was a big present in itself." Ryan pulled off Kellie's left mitten.

Kellie gasped when he slipped a beautiful diamond engagement ring onto her finger. "Whoa, when'd you get this?"

Ryan smiled. "At Christmas. Hannah and Gracie helped me pick it out. They said it had to be super special for Aunt Kellie."

Kellie's eyes filled with tears. It was. Even more so because her family shared in choosing it. Despite their problems, she had a family that loved her. And now, she'd become part of a new family who'd love her, too. The truth of that blessing humbled her.

She stared at the ring glittering in the light cast by streetlamps and Christmas lights and then she looked at Ryan. "Thank you."

He smiled. "Thank you for saying yes."

She laughed. "As if there would be any other answer."

He nodded his agreement and then they were pulled into more hugs from Dorrie and Hannah and even the folks watching nearby as they wished each other a Happy New Year.

This year promised to be a very good year, indeed.

* * * * *

Dear Reader,

Thank you for reading Ryan's and Kellie's journey to love and wholeness through their renewed faith in God. I hope you enjoyed it.

The first time Ryan showed up in *Season of Dreams* (Feb. 2011), I thought he'd be a really fun, tortured hero to write. Uh no—fun is not even close to describing Ryan's character development. I agonized over him, trying to find the right balance and the right heroine for him. And then along came Kellie Cavanaugh who formed before my eyes once I gave her the right name. Amazing what strength of character comes from a name. Kellie is perfect for Ryan because she understands him. As a strong person with emotional scars of her own, Kellie knew what Ryan was going through but was too afraid to love him. I think it took Ryan and Kellie to finally put their trust in God in a very real way to enable them to love each other perfectly.

God did not promise a life that would be easy, but He promised He'd never leave or forsake us. With the Creator of the Universe on our side, there's nothing we can't overcome.

Many Blessings,

Jenna

I love to hear from my readers. Please visit my website at www.jennamindel.com or drop me a note c/o Love Inspired Books, 233 Broadway, Suite 1001, New York, NY 10279.

Questions for Discussion

1. Like our earthly fathers, God promises to do what is best for us, including correction or punishment when needed. How is God's hand in Ryan's situation of forced counseling?

2. Have you ever read the poem "Hound of Heaven" by Francis Thompson? The opening lines show a man running from God. In what ways did Ryan also run from God?

3. Kellie worried about her immediate attraction to Ryan because of ethical concerns of getting personally involved with someone in counseling where she interned. Should she have been? Why or why not?

4. Ryan's estrangement from his brother was because Sinclair left him alone to grieve. Should Ryan have felt that way? Why? Why is it so easy to hold on to a grudge against a family member?

5. Kellie's past includes the self-destructive behavior of *cutting*. How has the church addressed this issue with their teens? How should they? How would you respond to a teenager who struggles with this?

6. When the book opens, Ryan is in denial regarding his grief over the death of his fiancée and his abuse of alcohol. When do you think Ryan accepted his alcoholism? Do you believe Ryan will succeed in his recovery? Why or why not?

7. Kellie keeps a tight rein on her feelings and steers clear of situations where she believes she may be emotionally hurt. Can you relate to that? In what ways?

8. How did Kellie show growth by the end of the book? What was the catalyst for Kellie giving a relationship with Ryan another chance?

9. In the New Living Bible translation, 1 Corinthians 13:7 reads: *Love never gives up, never loses faith, is always hopeful, and endures through every circumstance.* How did Kellie fall short of that when it came to Ryan? And what about her brother?

10. Ryan and Kellie work together on a house being built for a single mom in need. Are there any nonprofit organizations in your area that do this? How do you view what they do?

11. I usually end my books with a wedding scene as an epilogue, but didn't with this book. I chose an engagement scene instead. When and where do you think Ryan and Kellie will get married?

REQUEST YOUR FREE BOOKS!

2 FREE INSPIRATIONAL NOVELS
PLUS 2
FREE
MYSTERY GIFTS

Love Inspired

YES! Please send me 2 FREE Love Inspired® novels and my 2 FREE mystery gifts (gifts are worth about $10). After receiving them, if I don't wish to receive any more books, I can return the shipping statement marked "cancel." If I don't cancel, I will receive 6 brand-new novels every month and be billed just $4.74 per book in the U.S. or $5.24 per book in Canada. That's a saving of at least 21% off the cover price. It's quite a bargain! Shipping and handling is just 50¢ per book in the U.S. and 75¢ per book in Canada.* I understand that accepting the 2 free books and gifts places me under no obligation to buy anything. I can always return a shipment and cancel at any time. Even if I never buy another book, the two free books and gifts are mine to keep forever.   105/305 IDN F47Y

Name _____ (PLEASE PRINT)

Address _____ Apt. #

City _____ State/Prov. _____ Zip/Postal Code

Signature (if under 18, a parent or guardian must sign)

Mail to the **Harlequin® Reader Service:**
IN U.S.A.: P.O. Box 1867, Buffalo, NY 14240-1867
IN CANADA: P.O. Box 609, Fort Erie, Ontario L2A 5X3

**Are you a subscriber to Love Inspired books
and want to receive the larger-print edition?
Call 1-800-873-8635 or visit www.ReaderService.com.**

* Terms and prices subject to change without notice. Prices do not include applicable taxes. Sales tax applicable in N.Y. Canadian residents will be charged applicable taxes. Offer not valid in Quebec. This offer is limited to one order per household. Not valid for current subscribers to Love Inspired books. All orders subject to credit approval. Credit or debit balances in a customer's account(s) may be offset by any other outstanding balance owed by or to the customer. Please allow 4 to 6 weeks for delivery. Offer available while quantities last.

Your Privacy—The Harlequin® Reader Service is committed to protecting your privacy. Our Privacy Policy is available online at www.ReaderService.com or upon request from the Harlequin Reader Service.

We make a portion of our mailing list available to reputable third parties that offer products we believe may interest you. If you prefer that we not exchange your name with third parties, or if you wish to clarify or modify your communication preferences, please visit us at www.ReaderService.com/consumerchoice or write to us at Harlequin Reader Service Preference Service, P.O. Box 9062, Buffalo, NY 14269. Include your complete name and address.

LI13R

"I can't undo what I did." She leaned back against the wall
and with her fingers pinched the bridge of her nose. Soft
blond hair framed her face.

"No, you can't." He guessed he didn't need to tell her
what an understatement that was. She'd robbed him. She'd
robbed Lindsey. Come to think of it, she'd robbed his entire
family. Lindsey's family.

Jana's shoulder started to shake. Her body sagged against
the wall and her knees buckled. He grabbed her, holding her
close as she sobbed into his shoulder. She still fit perfectly
and he didn't want that. He didn't want to remember how it
had been when they were young. He didn't want her scent
to be familiar or her touch to be the touch he missed.

It all came back to him, holding her. He pushed it away
by remembering coming home to an empty house and a note.

He held her until her sobs became quieter, her body
ceased shaking. He held her and he tried hard not to think
about the years he'd spent searching, wishing things could
have been different for them, wishing she'd come back.

"Mrs. Cooper?"

He realized he was still holding Jana, his hands stroking
her hair, comforting her. His hands dropped to his sides and

she stepped back, visibly trying to regain her composure. She managed a shaky smile.

"She'll be fine," he assured the woman in the white lab coat, who was walking toward them, her gaze lingering on Jana.

"I'm Nurse Bonnie Palmer. If you could join me in the conference room, we'll discuss what needs to happen next for your daughter."

Jana shook her head. "I'm going to stay with Lindsey."

Blake gave her a strong look and pushed back a truckload of suspicion. She wasn't going anywhere with Lindsey. Not now. He knew that and he'd fight through the doubts about Jana and her motives. He'd do what he had to do to make sure Lindsey got the care she needed.

He'd deal with his ex-wife later.

He's committed to helping his daughter, but can Blake Cooper ever trust the wife who broke his heart?

Pick up THE COWBOY'S REUNITED FAMILY *to find out. Available February 2014 wherever Love Inspired® Books are sold.*

LIEXP0114